VINCE FOSTER:

MOONSHOT

BOOK ONE

AUSTIN WINDSOR

Cover design by Miblart

ISBN 978-1-7391528-6-4

www.austinwindsor.co.uk

For Chaz, for being so good at selling these when you
worked at the bookshop

PROLOGUE

22 APRIL 1983

"No, I'm sorry," the presenter relented. "Please, go on."

"Well, the fact is that there are individuals within our government who would not hesitate to plunge our nation, and, heavens, the entire world, into nuclear war. Of that I have no doubts, and the same goes for the Soviets, too. Think back to, for example, the Cuban Crisis—we had ships surrounding Cuba on the seemingly fabled hopes that the Russians wouldn't retaliate at this act of, to put it quite frankly, war—President Kennedy wasn't fooling anyone by his use of the word quarantine. What happened was a blockade, not—"

"Wait a minute," the presenter interrupted. "Are you suggesting it was a bad idea to force the Soviets to take their missiles off an island not even a hundred miles from American soil?"

"It was the closest we've ever been to nuclear war and it was an incredibly risky manoeuvre. Everyone knows the immediate effect of a nuclear strike, but I don't think the extent of catastrophe is ever really discussed. There's the destruction, yes. Whole cities turned to dust. If you're in the blast zone, you're turned into a shadow on the sidewalk. Vaporised. And then there's the radiation. If you live close enough to the site of the blast but you're unfortunate enough to survive the shockwave, you spend weeks dying a slow, gruesome death.

"But war isn't one bomb. War is many bombs. There's this new theory about what's being called nuclear winter. You see, the idea with nuclear war is to target dense, urban centres for maximum destruction. Very effective as far as strategy goes. Drop a thermonuclear bomb on a metropolis and it will burn to the ground. Soot from the destruction will stream into the sky and saturate the atmosphere with this matter that reflects sunlight. You've heard of global warming? This would be the reverse. Now imagine an all-out war between two global superpowers, dropping bombs on city after city after city. Aside from the senseless deaths from the blasts, there would be far wider ramifications that go on to affect not just the belligerents in the conflict but the entire world.

"All this soot ends up in the sky, blocking the sun. What happens then? Agricultural failure. Suddenly, countries which provide the world with huge proportions of its food lose their entire harvests. People go hungry. Starvation takes place in countries where such a concept has been fallacy for the past... God knows how many years. This

2

leads quickly to civil unrest. And what's always quick to follow uncontained civil unrest? Political upheaval. You can forget the status quo, because the governments of the day will be forced to radically overhaul the way they do business or they will be overthrown. Much of the world would fall into anarchy. Brutal conflicts would take place in order to secure what's left of the food supply for one population, leaving everyone else to die off.

"This is the reality of nuclear war. It wouldn't just wipe out two belligerent sides. It would wipe out order as we know it. In most places, anyways. We're very resilient creatures and we've survived terrible catastrophes before, but society would never be the same."

The presenter leaned forwards in his chair, mirroring the intense curiosity exhibited by the members of the studio audience off camera. "What do you mean by that?"

"I mean either total reorganisation or utter collapse. When I talk about the death and destruction caused by nuclear winter, I don't mean millions of people would die. I mean billions. And we would have to adapt to it."

CHAPTER 1

80 YEARS LATER

"Here for Mr Maddox."

The woman at the reception desk took one quick glance at the man standing expectantly but patiently before her. He didn't stand out from some of the usual high-brow clients. He wore his dark hair in neat curtains. A tailored black shirt and trousers complemented his lean, slightly muscular figure. And if that wasn't brooding enough, he wore a black trench coat over the top of it to boot.

"Could I get your name, please?" she asked distractedly.

"He knows I'm here for him. Thirteen-thirty on the dot. That's when I'm expected. And that's what time it is."

"I'm sorry, I just don't have a booking—"

"If you're harassing a visitor, Molly, your hours are going to be extended," a man's voice sounded over an intercom on the desk. "Send him up."

"O-of course, sir. Right away," she stammered, pressing a button on the intercom to respond. Finally, her eyes returned to Vince, and she nodded in the direction of a lift at the side of the lobby.

"Seventieth floor," she said quietly.

"Thank you." Vince nodded casting a wary eye around the rest of the lobby and instinctively making a mental note of the security cameras' locations as he turned away. He had already taken notice of a pair of armed guards stood adjacent to the entrance on the inside when he came in. Anything else the lobby offered in the way of security was either hidden or absent.

The clear glass door slid open on his approach. "Seventy," he said as it closed.

It would have been very easy for Vince to feel small in the excessive grandeur of the offices of the Camden Space Corporation, but he hadn't come of his own accord. He had been invited.

The lift began to move as soon as he had spoken and he ran a smoothing hand over the creases in his coat during the twenty seconds it took to arrive. He wasn't nervous, and his expression remained still. The doors did not open by themselves, though Vince could see the shadowed outline of Oliver Maddox, and Oliver Maddox had seen him. He pressed a button on his desk and the doors opened, Vince stepping slowly into the expansive office of the CEO of the Camden Space Corporation. The entire back wall behind Maddox's desk was constructed from glass, and shelves filled with various trinkets and ornaments lined the walls extending from the entrance to the lift.

"Come on, take a seat," Maddox said impatiently. "We haven't got all day."

"I don't know what you're expecting from me, Mr Maddox, but it will take time, whatever it is," Vince said. "So I should hope we do have all day."

"Oh, really? I think you'll find this is my office and we're on my schedule, not yours." Maddox forced a smile, standing up and extending a hand towards Vince. "Can I interest you in anything? Cocaine? Heroin?"

"No, thank you." Vince waved a hand in front of his face. "I'm happy enough with sims."

"I've tried them, you know, and it just isn't as good as the real thing. Have you ever been high? Like, actually high, rather than simulated."

"The neural chips are supposed to trigger the same impulses as real substances. So the marketers say."

"They're full of shit. You can't beat a real high." Maddox produced a vial of white powder from a drawer under his desk and arranged it into a line with a credit card. Vince glanced at the details on it, and the expiry date read *11/36*.

"That's a relic," he commented as Maddox's head recoiled back. "How come you keep that knocking around?"

Maddox slammed his fists against the table and brought himself forward. "Ah, I like old tech and whatnot. I mean, we've been paying with our phones since way before the war, but I miss physical cards. There's just something about them."

"I don't think I've ever had one."

"I can imagine. How old are you? Twenty-seven, twenty-eight?"

"I'll take that as a compliment," Vince laughed. "Thirty-four."

"Fucking hell, what do you use for your skin? And your hair, so luscious!" Maddox kicked his feet up onto the desk and ran a hand through his own greying hair.

"I don't do anything to it, actually. Apart from not spending much time in the sunlight, so I don't tan. War obviously made that a lot easier for a while."

"Yes, yes it did. You see those smokestacks over there?"

Maddox whirled around in his chair and gestured ambiguously to the various skyscrapers, factories, and compounds comprising the northern London skyline. Vince assumed Maddox meant what looked to be a power station at its centre. The sky was overcast, and a thin carpet of grey smog made distinction difficult.

"Do you remember when they used to tell us we had to stop burning that stuff? And now we have to burn it so that the temperature doesn't *drop* too much. Scientists. Can never trust them."

"I don't suppose the climate scientists pre-war were calculating for the effects of nuclear winter."

"No, I suppose not. Well, pleasantries exchanged, shall we get down to business?"

"Let's."

Maddox turned back from gazing out of the window and looked Vince in the eyes for so long that Vince would have thought he was flirting.

"Maria spoke very highly of you," he said. "Remarkable, really, that you were able to impress her so much. I don't think I've ever heard her so thrilled."

"What can I say?" Vince raised his eyebrows and shrugged. "I set out to do a job and I did it."

Maria Sanchez was Vince's contact in the American government. As secretary of state, she wielded a great deal of power and was very close to the President. The little respect she did hold for people was reserved for select few, a list Vince had joined when he had assassinated a political rival of hers several years beforehand.

"So cleanly, though, and without the faintest trace. President didn't even need to interfere in the investigation. It's not easy to do that, nowadays. Yet you manage it."

The conversation paused and Maddox took the opportunity to inhale another line of cocaine.

"Here's my offer, Mr Foster. You're aware that I've got competitors. I need you to change that. New Orion—I want the whole board of directors dead. All six of them. And to top it off, the chief engineer. You think you could do that?"

"Please, call me Vince." The hitman straightened his hair. "And it depends."

"On?"

"A number of factors. I'm sure you're aware of the largest."

"Cheeky sod." Maddox chuckled and retrieved a tablet from his desk, tapping away until he found what he was looking for. "I think it will be worth it for you. Twenty million U.S. dollars, cash. I would have paid you in euros, but... you know."

Vince feigned neutrality in his reaction but was secretly brimming with excitement. His last contract had by no means been low-profile, and for it he had received one million dollars. Any remaining doubts he had had about the offer swiftly evaporated.

"And where is this money coming from that twenty million dollars can just... disappear from an account without anyone batting an eye? It has to be untraceable," Vince cautioned.

"Don't worry." Maddox's face contorted suddenly and the polite façade that had previously existed was replaced by an unsettling arrogance. "I fucking own this city, alright? Twenty million dollars is chump change. An accounting error. My accountants are such stupid fucking cretins anyways that it's to be expected."

Vince's composure remained unchanged, though he was internally taken aback. "The other oligarchs will have their eyes on you."

"I'm sorry, but I don't need a fucking lecture about how to do my business. I'm hiring you to do a job, Vince. The context is irrelevant to you."

"On the contrary. As I'm sure you can understand, I have to be very careful not to take a contract that will end up with me ambushed by the police in a sting, or with my name on somebody's kill list. You're very powerful, of course, but there are others in the City of London who are as well. And not just London. With a contract like this, I've got the American, European, and Chinese governments watching the situation. And then there will be corporate spies from Yamiyo. Absolutely nothing about this allows me to be careless about the context. The context is everything."

Maddox snorted and reached into his desk, retrieving a cigar. He cut off its head with a tool on his desk and lit it with an ornately decorated lighter.

"I don't suppose you want one of these, either." He glanced up at Vince, who shook his head.

"Just so we're clear, I want to do this job," Vince clarified. "But I have to be careful. In fact, I wouldn't be surprised if those three governments I mentioned are monitoring this very building. My name is probably already on their radar."

Maddox sucked on his cigar and then released a thick ring of smoke which dispersed against the ceiling.

"Nobody knows anything about our meeting, other than me, you, and Molly. Molly is not a spy, not for the Americans, the Chinese, the Europeans, or the Japanese. She's a dumb bimbo I hired as eye candy. And unless you think, you know, I'm a spy, then you have nothing to worry about. This room is protected by transmission blockers. It is scoured for bugs on a weekly basis. Any downloads are manually screened by a team I have down on the thirty-second floor before being passed along to me. We're vigilant when it comes to cyber security at the CSC. And as for physical security? I have cameras watching every square inch of land in a five-mile radius. I have my own PIs look-

ing for hostile PIs. With the press of a button—*this* button"—he pointed to a physical button built into his desk—
"I can have the whole place put on lockdown. Doors lock,
lifts stop, alarms sound. My private security force then
comes in, and they're no ordinary mercenaries. They're
equipped with *military*-grade weapons, and most of them
I hired straight out of the SAS when they got bored of the
pittance they got paid to work in the UR. That is the context, Vince. Now, may we move onto the details of the
job?"

Vince had held eye contact for the entirety of Maddox's
monologue and he kept it that way as he nodded his affirmation.

"Good. Let's start with you. Tell me what you think you
need."

"Private transport. I need to get into the country and
around it undetected and unregistered."

"You can use my private jet. I need to visit Maria soon
anyways. And I've got plenty of cars waiting."

"I can't use a car you already own. It needs to be new,
or owned by someone who isn't linked to you in any way."

Maddox rolled his eyes and sighed. "You're paranoid,
you know that?"

"I'm a professional," Vince responded unwaveringly.

"Right, fine, we can sort a car. Multiple, if you want."

"I do want. I'll likely need a new one for each kill."

"It's done. What about weapons?"

"I'll use my own. What's more important to me is data—
I want information about these people. Who they are,

their relationships, their daily routines. I need to know as much as possible about them."

"Half of them have got fucking Wikipedia pages. Look it up."

"Not enough. If you don't have information about them, I will need to spend time discovering it myself." Vince finally broke eye contact, looking to the side as he smirked. "And that costs extra. And how do you want these people to die? Do you want it to be quiet? Do you want them to disappear? Or can their cars explode?"

"I want them disappeared," Maddox said coldly. "That's non-negotiable."

"In which case the data is all the more important. So, do you have anything for me to work with? Or will I have to find it out myself?"

Maddox sighed again. "I've got profiles with their names, addresses, all that. But I don't know what they eat for dinner every fucking night."

"Then I'm afraid this job is going to take a lot longer and cost a lot more," Vince said. "But we can cut the time significantly if we employ help."

"Help?"

"A good friend and colleague of mine, Noah Cox. He's done plenty of missions with me, and he's about the most reliable person I know. I can delegate some of the targets to him, and he will do just as good a job as me, I assure you of that. And you won't have to pay him any more—it will come out of my share."

"Whatever methods you use to take them out—I don't give a rat's arse. Hire the fucking Wagner Group for all I care. As long as it's quiet and can't be traced back to me."

"Understood. Well, I'd like to see one of these profiles. Can I have a look?"

Maddox exhaled another expertly formed smoke ring before setting down the cigar to lean against a glass ashtray. He unlocked the tablet from earlier and swiped through various screens before finally finding one of the profiles and handing the device to Vince.

Name: Ellie Sunarav. DOB: 24/03/96. Address: 30 Main St, Apt 11B, Brooklyn, NY 11201.

"Is this really all you have?" He skimmed over some other irrelevant personal details and a brief description of her personality and biography, only interested in her address and portrait image at the top-left of the document. He attempted to scroll, expecting at least a second page, but found nothing.

"Like I told you, I don't know what they're having for dinner. Forgive my *ignorance*, but for everyone else I've had offed, this has been enough. You're by far the whiniest hitman I've ever hired."

"I can tell you categorically every other hitman you've hired has been too terrified to say to your face that you don't give them enough. This is pitiful. I've got my work cut out for me."

"I'm paying you twenty million fucking dollars for it! You should fucking expect to have your work cut out for you!"

"Thirty," Vince retorted. "Twenty for the elimination. Ten for the tracking and documenting."

"You have got some bollocks on you." Maddox picked up his cigar and took a long drag.

"Nobody else will be able to provide the results you're after. You hire someone else and they'll jump with joy after you tell them how much you'll pay them and accept without hesitation. Then they'll fly off to New York and get themselves killed when they act with greedy haste and without adequate preparation."

Maddox leaned back in his chair and produced a third smoke ring, the largest yet.

"Fine," he conceded. "But on the condition—"

"That it won't be traceable," Vince interrupted, meeting his gaze as he sat back up in his chair. "Not a speck of evidence that could lead back to you. Not a single image of my face on even a millisecond of security footage. Not a single fingerprint on a single doorhandle. This is the service I offer."

"You talk a big game, Vince," Maddox chuckled. "I look forward to seeing whether it turns into results."

"It will." Vince rose from his chair and extended a hand, which Maddox met with the same firmness as at their greeting. "Keep an eye on the papers."

CHAPTER 2

Noah Cox, like Vince, lived in the City of London, if only
for the fact that it meant they paid no taxes of any kind. In
fact, they were neighbours. Noah lived in a flat on the
thirty-third floor of a high-rise overlooking Hyde Park,
while Vince owned a more modest house between it and
what used to be the French embassy. The two, when they
happened to be at home at the same time, would go out in
the morning for a run through the park before the sun
rose, which was their most private opportunity to talk
about work.

"Oliver Maddox? *The* Oliver Maddox?" Noah asked be-
wilderedly as they turned right to run along the waterside.

"He's a right bastard," Vince said.

When they weren't out for a run, they even dressed the same, just with a different colour scheme. While Vince chose to clad himself in full black, Noah wore browns complementing a trench coat in khaki. But unlike Vince, he wore glasses, with black rectangular frames to complement his ruthlessly ovular face.

"And he heard about you from who? Maria?"

Vince nodded, refraining from talking as they passed a pair of dogwalkers before carrying on.

"You have to tell me about the meeting, come on," Noah implored. "What was his office like?"

"Quite plain, actually. Aside from these shelves just rammed full of useless junk that might have had some value to him. Either that or it was to show off."

"And what about him? What was he like?"

"I told you. A right bastard. Invited me in and first thing he did was snort a line. Two minutes later he snorted a second."

"Why doesn't he just use a sim? It triggers the same impulses!"

"Some bullshit about the 'real thing' being better. He then went on to smoke a cigar, which fucking reeked. It was all worth it though, because you'll never guess how much he's paying me."

"I don't know what the job is. Tell me that, first, at least, so I can get an idea of the ballpark."

Vince cast a quick glance up and down the path and then waited until they had run to a clear stretch of path free of brush along its edges.

"The entire New Orion board of directors plus the chief engineer," he whispered. Noah's eyes expanded and he shook his head as they ran past a sculpture and took a left to diverge from the waterside.

"That's big, Vince, even for you," he finally said.

"Go on, have a guess. How much do you think?"

"Oh, God. Five million? I mean that's only reasonable, right?"

Vince said nothing, instead pointing up and grinning.

"Oh, shit! Ten?"

"Thirty," Vince said.

Noah snorted amusedly as they turned to run around the Princess Diana Memorial Fountain, remaining speechless as they sped up to overtake another runner.

"I need your help, though, so some of it could be yours," Vince admitted.

"Seven targets? You'll need more than just me, mate. This sounds like a three-person job, minimum."

"It's too high risk for anyone else. You're the only person I trust with it."

"I'm touched, but we'll need more help. Come back to mine for breakfast and we'll chat more about it. I have a few ideas."

Vince told a lot of white lies in his line of work but his declaration of trust in Noah was a steadfast truth. The pair had known each other since Noah was only a teenager, and Vince had only just graduated from King's College, having studied a degree that would go on to serve him exactly zero times in his adult life. He was instead trained as a hitman by his uncle, and met Noah at an open day for the very same university he had shunned. He had agreed to attend only to try to dissuade potential students and Noah was the only one to give him the time of day. The rest was history.

Ten years later and they shared an unbreakable bond. They had been partners on innumerable contracts and been each other's saving graces in several near-death situations. Vince trusted him more than he trusted his wife—and spent more time with him, too.

The pair spent the rest of their run in relative silence, looping around over a bridge and heading back towards a cut-through exit which led practically to the front door of Noah's high-rise.

Hyde Park's continued survival was a lasting miracle that Vince attributed to the oligarch Cressida Hart's ownership of Kensington Palace following the dissolution of the monarchy. That was only one small part of the complete political upheaval that unfolded after the 2044 Indo-Pakistani War went nuclear. In the view over all of London Vince and Noah had as they whizzed up to the thirty-third floor in the glass-walled lift, the sun beginning to peek over the horizon, the park was the only visible patch of green against a paradoxical congregation of greys and neon lights.

"Morning, my love," Noah exclaimed as the opaque glass door to his flat slid open in anticipation of his arrival. His girlfriend, a woman called Ruth Jones, was already up and milling around in the kitchen. She smiled and pulled Noah in for an embrace as they arrived before politely greeting Vince as well.

Ruth was lovely in every way and Vince always felt terrible for the fact that Noah had never been able to be truthful with her about his profession. She was convinced he was a photographer, a charade he was able to maintain owing to his genuine passion for it as a hobby. Evidence was visible all around his home—the walls were covered in all manner of his best shots, from nature to landscapes, street to fashion. Vince sometimes joked that he should stop lying about it being his career and pursue it for real.

"Did you want anything to eat, Vince?" Ruth called as Vince made his way into their living room.

"Oh, no, thank you. I'd love to use your shower, though."

"You know you don't have to ask, moron," Noah said.

Vince chuckled and continued on into the bathroom, which was almost as large as his bedroom in his own house. He had warned Noah in the past about living beyond his means and arousing suspicion, but it had turned out that Ruth worked as Chief Security Officer at one of the city's biggest banks and brought in more than enough to cover the entire cost of the flat with her own salary.

The shower detected Vince and assigned itself to his usual preset as he stripped himself out of his sweat-sodden running clothes and tossed them into the laundry chute.

He stepped into the shower, listening to music with his neural chip as robotic arms appeared from the walls and massaged shampoo into his hair and shower gel over his body. The water then continued to run for exactly five minutes before the ceiling opened up to unveil an oversized fan which produced what felt like enough force to topple a tree. His body was mostly dry, at which point a smaller fan held by one of the robotic arms appeared from the wall and set about drying his hair with a stream of hot air. When he thought about it all, Vince snorted, grinning, and shook his head.

He stepped out of the shower to find an outfit waiting for him, set out on racks by drones that filtered constantly in and out of the bathroom. He pulled on a shirt, trousers, and belt, all black. His trench coat and boots waiting in the cloakroom were black, too.

A plate with a croissant and a cup of tea were forced into his hands as he left the bathroom and Noah walked away before he could protest. They sat down in front of the television in the living room, the wall to their left constructed from complete glass reminiscent of Oliver Maddox's office. Drones could be seen taking off in droves as the neon lights all switched off with the rising sun and people began to flood into the streets below, unmoving traffic having already assembled on the roads.

"Let's see what new tragedy they've got to spin today, then," Noah said, pointing to the television. The embedded seventy-inch screen turned on and flicked automatically onto BBC News, where the pair watched a report about a European plan for a new moon mining station.

"Do you still pay for this crap?" Vince commented, flitting his eyes away from the television and onto his phone screen, where he swiped away a message from his wife.

"It may lack the impartiality it had twenty years ago but it's better than the alternative."

"I just don't watch the news. You'll be much happier that way."

"I don't know, Vince, you don't seem like the picture of mental health. You ought to take a break every now and again."

"And do what? Stew? Sit at home and be forced to deal with my wife? I think I'd rather stick forks in my eyes."

"You need a hobby," Ruth chimed in. "There must be something you enjoy doing in your spare time."

"He doesn't have any spare time," Noah exclaimed. "All he does is work."

"Perhaps you ought to learn a thing or two," Ruth teased. "I'm joking, of course, darling. It would be lovely to have you here more often."

"Well, I'd love to be here more often. But as it happens, I might be away for a little while. We've just had ourselves a big offer. Actually, I can't take the credit. It's all Vince."

That was another part of the lie they fed Ruth, and in extension Vince's wife. Noah was the photographer, and Vince his manager with all the connections.

"Oh, really?" Ruth's eyes lit up. "Go on, do tell."

Noah looked at Vince and raised his eyebrows expectantly.

"It's a big corporate job in America," Vince explained. "At the behest of Oliver Maddox."

"Oliver Maddox?" Ruth's jaw dropped and she clapped her hands excitedly. "You're not pulling my leg here, are you?"

"Vince has friends in the American government, for God's sake," Noah said. "Maddox is nothing for him."

"Maddox pays more than any of my friends in the American government," Vince said, sipping his tea. "But it's not exactly my doing that landed me so many influential contacts. That's all on my uncle."

"God rest his soul."

"Oh, I am so very happy for you. The both of you," Ruth beamed. "You will have to tell me more about it later. I'm going into the office early today. I'm off to the shower—it's nice to see you, Vince."

"And you, Ruth."

Ruth finished the last bite of her croissant and placed the plate on a waiting robot, which promptly wheeled away to the kitchen where they heard it loading the dishwasher. She then departed and they heard the shower start up shortly thereafter, at a much lower intensity than was Vince's preference.

Noah leaned in and his voice fell hushed. "I recently did a mission in Bristol with this Serbian guy—"

"No Europeans," Vince said firmly.

"Yep, fair enough. What about a Japanese—"

"Silly suggestion. Might I make it clear that they can't be from London, America, Europe, China, or Japan?"

"That narrows down my choices a bit... hmm..."

Noah unlocked his phone, brow furrowed, and flicked through a list of contacts.

"How about this—Hamzah Al-Habib. He's Moroccan, and young. Only twenty-one."

"How the hell do you know him, then?"

"Freak coincidence. We both got hired by the same person to kill some Spanish politician, a high-up in the federal government. He did tell me that he'd hired someone else already, but neglected to tell me that he hadn't actually sacked him. Hamzah and I nearly killed each other when we turned up to the guy's doorstep at the same time. It was a real bonding experience, actually, making our buyer pay us both double."

"You know the next question. Can I trust him?"

"Definitely. Like I said, he's young, so he's got less connections. He's Moroccan, like I also said, so no ties to the United or Federated States. Definitely not got anything to do with the Chinese or Japanese, and he told me he's never even been to London."

"How's he on the job so young?"

"There are schools for it there. Set up maybe ten years after the war. He went to one of them, and he excelled."

Vince pursed his lips in consideration and sipped slowly at his tea, which was going cold.

"I can call him up if you want. You can have a chat with him personally."

"I'd rather meet him in person. And not in a virtual environment."

"I'm sure he'd be interested. Do you want me to send him a message?"

Vince deliberated over the delivery of his answer and there was a period of quiet filled only with the gentle drumming of water from the bathroom and the ambient rambling of the newsreader on the television.

"Do you not know anyone else?"

"Do *you* not? You've been at this longer than I have. You must have contacts."

That was one regard in which Vince faltered. When it came to his work, he was very effective at its physical practice, but he usually opted to work alone. If Noah was unavailable, he always opted to work alone.

"Not any other hitmen," he admitted.

"So shy. You need to let me take you out more."

"I go out plenty. I work fine on my own or with you. I don't need anyone else."

"Except for right now."

"Stop being pedantic. Do you know anyone else who could do it, or not?"

Noah sighed, rolling his eyes and flicking back through the list of contacts. He stopped for a minute, looking as if he was going to ask a question, but then didn't.

"Considering you've ruled out anyone from most of the stable world, I don't, no. Hamzah is our best option from outside of... well, yeah, most of the stable world."

The sound of the water in the shower came to a stop before being promptly replaced by the much louder whirring of the fan.

"We need someone, Vince. Nobody will be perfect. Hamzah's our best bet."

"Alright," Vince relented. "What's his number?"

"I'll send you his contact. He's in Germany right now, doing a job for Deutsche Bank. But I'll let him know you want to get in touch."

The ceiling fan switched off and the quieter hairdryer switched on.

"I hope he can clear his calendar, because I'm flying to New York. You, however, you've got your pick. Do you want L.A., Sacramento, or D.C.?"

"Don't any of them live anywhere that isn't a wasteland?" Noah complained.

"Yep, but I've taken those ones for myself."

"You're going to New York. That's evidently not the case," he mulled. "I'll start with L.A., I suppose."

"You can do Sacramento as well, then. I'll forward you the details I got from Maddox," Vince agreed, his voice speeding up as the hairdryer fell silent. He swigged the rest of his tea and then headed for the door, sliding on his boots and slipping into his trench coat. "I'll see you later, Noah. Don't fuck it up."

Vince heard the door to the bathroom slide open and marched out of the flat without a moment's hesitation.

CHAPTER 3

Vince stepped into the lift and issued a command to go down to the garage, where he had parked his car, a beat-up Mercedes S-Class he had to fuel with biodiesel after global oil production dried up around fifteen years prior. It was expensive stuff, but that wasn't a concern for Vince.

It took fifteen minutes to make it onto the street from the garage door with the constant flow of pedestrians and the gridlock on the road. It was then an hour's agonising drive to Heathrow, where one of Oliver Maddox's private jets awaited.

During the six-hour flight Vince was presented with a greater selection of alcoholic beverages than would have been available in the average bar. He rejected them all in favour of a cup of Earl Grey, of which he made swift work before delving into research on his first target by browsing the internet through his neural chip. After several hours, he then decided to rest and set himself to sleep.

He woke up as the plane touched down on the runway at JFK and was transferred directly from the plane into a helicopter, landing five minutes later at the top of a sky-scraper about the height of the Empire State Building. Vince was led yet again by more faceless gun-wielding security forces down into the building before finally being shown into a flat, where they departed.

The flat was larger than any he had ever seen and left nothing to wish for in the way of gadgetry. Every single wall, barring that hosting the door, was a window, but with a single vocal command he could cause them to go translucent or even a completely solid colour of his choice. He opted for a relatively strong opacity so that the city sights were still present behind the blurred filter, but any attempt to see into the flat was futile.

"Hello, Mr Foster," a woman's voice said.

Vince pulled his gun, a silenced Heckler and Koch MK 23, out of his concealed holster and spun around, aiming it between the woman's eyes. He then sighed, closing his eyes, and holstered the weapon before marching into the study, the woman following closely behind.

"If this is Maddox's idea of a joke, I'm not interested," Vince said curtly, sitting down at the desk—twice the size of that in his usual office—and powering on the computer.

"I am your personal assistant," she said, placing a cold hand on his shoulder.

"I don't want a personal assistant." Vince batted her hand away and was greeted by the setup screen that Maddox had told him to expect in a message sent to his phone while he was asleep on the plane.

"Mr Maddox ensures that all those he works with do so in the utmost comfort."

"You're not making me comfortable. Now get out, or I'll shoot you in the head. Would that destroy who you are? Or is your personality stored remotely? They do still keep storage chips in the head, don't they?"

"I'm remotely stored, but I would certainly be put out of action if you were to shoot me. Not to mention it would be very expensive and Mr Maddox would not be pleased."

"I don't give a shit, I didn't ask for an android. Get out."

"I will give you some time alone," the woman conceded.

Vince released a sigh of relief and turned his attention back to the computer screen where he finished setting up and was presented with a collection of documents pertaining to the targets. In terms of information Maddox had collected, it was just as limited as the day they had met, although there were some links for additional reading.

He clicked through to the folder relevant to Ellie Sunarav and read through the same information he already knew. A few pictures provided nothing of particular value, the only thing to stand out being her extravagant fashion sense. Lists of known associates contained information he had already found during the flight and he let out a sigh of frustration as he gave up on the material provided and went to make a cup of tea.

His phone vibrated as he entered the kitchen, the kettle already boiling, and he picked it up while he searched the cupboards for a mug. The screen read *No Caller ID* and he left it to go to voicemail.

A buzz almost a minute later, Vince having successfully located a mug, indicated a voicemail had been left. He left the tea to brew as he walked into the living room, turning the windows transparent and gazing over the city.

"Mr Foster," the message began. Vince immediately recognised an accent. "My name is Hamzah. I know you were not expecting this call, but I thought it would be best to reach out to you sooner rather than later."

Really, Noah? You gave him my number? Vince thought.

"Noah Cox explained to me that you had a possible job for me. I am making this call to let you know that I unfortunately am not currently looking for work. But I appreciate Noah's recommendation, and I hope that we will work together in the future, at a more practicable time. Thank you."

Forgetting about his tea, Vince called Noah and paced restlessly back and forth in front of the glass wall.

"Yes?" Noah answered after several rings.

"Two things. One—why did you give Hamzah my number?"

"I thought I'd let him show a bit of initiative. I take it he did as much?"

"Yeah. That leads me to our second thing. He doesn't want the work. Doesn't even know what it is, unless you were enough of a cretin to tell him that as well. He's too busy."

"Too busy?" Noah gasped in amusement. "That can't be right."

"I'm calling him back now and if he doesn't respond, I'm never speaking to him again."

"Now wait, Vince, wait." Vince could visualise the exact hand gestures Noah was making on the other end of the phone. "We can't do it without him. There'll be too much suspicion. If you tell him what the work actually is, he'll do it. I don't see any reason why he wouldn't."

"I hope you're right. I'll see you in a bit, Noah."

He ended the call and returned to the kitchen to find his tea coloured an enticing dark brown. He couldn't find any milk in the fridge as he looked through his contacts on his phone for Hamzah's number and became increasingly frustrated as he pored over the entire kitchen.

"May I be of any assistance, Mr Foster?" the android appeared and Vince's hand again went straight for his gun. It wasn't the first time he had seen an android, but it was by far the most realistic he had ever encountered.

"Yes, actually. Where the hell do I get some milk around here?" He found Hamzah's number in his phone and pressed call.

"It is dispensed from the coffee machine. May I handle your drink for you?"

"No, you may not." Vince lowered his mug under the tap, only to crane his neck and find there were two, in distinctly different locations. The phone continued to ring as he explored the options presented to him on the coffee machine's screen, noting that none of them related to tea. Another ring. He finally found the options pertaining exclusively to milk and muttered annoyedly to himself as he found that 'a splash' wasn't an option when it came to volume. Another ring, and the phone fell silent.

"Bastard," Vince said, cursing both at Hamzah's failure to pick up and the overflow of milk into his mug as he accidentally keyed in an extra zero to the measurement. "Robot, make me a cup of tea. A splash of milk. No, I don't know what that is in millilitres. Work it out."

He called Hamzah again and anxiously paced back into the living room. Again, he received no answer and tried for a third time.

"If I may recommend, Mr Foster, some stress-reducing exercises may be of benefit to you." The android appeared from the kitchen clutching a steaming mug. "Your blood pressure is currently uncharacteristically high. Do you frequently practice meditation?"

"How long did you brew that for? Thirty seconds? Do it again, you useless scrap heap," Vince said irritably as the phone fell silent once more. The android nodded and exited in silence.

Vince rubbed his forehead with his palms and took a deep breath, setting the phone down on the glass table occupying the centre of the living room between three adjacent sofas, each sporting a minimalistic geometric design in white. They weren't particularly comfortable when he took a seat.

"TV. Go to CNN," Vince said. The television, which must have been ninety inches at the least, flared immediately to life and displayed the Maddox Group logo before switching to CNN. Over the drone of the news anchor, he stared agitatedly at his phone on the table and forced himself to resist the urge to call again. The android returned after several minutes with a cup of tea a pleasantly surprising shade of brown, and at a temperature just right to drink straight away.

Vince had picked up the phone before the first ring had even concluded and it took all his willpower not to immediately answer it. He waited for three rings and then brought it to his ear in anticipation.

"Hello?" he asked, sounding nonchalant.

"Mr Foster? I'm sorry, I was momentarily predisposed. Did you get my message?"

"I did, Hamzah—may I call you Hamzah?"

"Please."

"And you can call me Vince. Yes, I received your message. I wanted to make it very clear, as Noah has seemingly failed to do so himself—this is not an opportunity you want to pass up." There was a pause as Vince waited expectantly for some sort of response. "Are you still with me?"

"Tell me more. What does the job entail?"

"I can't give you any specifics until you sign some forms, you know that. Except for your reward." Another pause, which Hamzah again failed to fill. "Five million dollars for two people. Do I have your attention?"

"You do. My schedule has become suddenly clear. Where am I to meet you? And when?"

"New York City. I'll call you back in a bit with more instructions as to the address. But it will be tomorrow. I have some work to do tonight."

"Very well. Thank you for the opportunity, Vince."

Hamzah had hung up before Vince had pulled the phone away from his ear and he looked at the device with a strange sense of awe. "Cocky bastard," he muttered before, relaxedly, finishing his cup of tea as he watched the news.

He made another call to Oliver Maddox to arrange transport for Hamzah and then headed down to the garage in the basement of the apartment block. There he was greeted by another android who introduced him to an array of cars from myriad different manufacturers.

"Mr Maddox has instructed that you may choose any of these. It is entirely up to you," the android droned.

The cars lining the left-hand side of the garage were flashy, high-performance supercars. They must have cost seven figures each. Driving one was out of the question.

Those on the right-hand side of the garage were more modest. Vince traced his eyes over an Audi saloon, a BMW SUV, and decided against both owing to their colour and size respectively. He finally settled upon a hydrogen-powered Toyota Corolla in humble silver. The android handed over the keys and he drove off into the streets he had known on so many occasions before.

CHAPTER 4

Main Street in Brooklyn wasn't far. Traffic made a ten-mile journey into an hour, but that was to be expected. The building to which Vince arrived he already knew well from his research—the Sweeney Building, built in 1910. A charming condo with clear views of the Manhattan skyline and individual apartment prices averaging more than thirty million dollars. His target did not live modestly.

Vince parked on the adjacent street and reached into his bag, pulling out a pollution mask and a pair of sunglasses. He wasn't going to be able to socially engineer his way through the lobby of the Sweeney Building, but there was a seafood restaurant next door. That, he had decided, was his way in.

The restaurant had just opened when he stepped up to the entrance and he was greeted by a fresh-faced server with authentically American enthusiasm.

"Welcome to the Ivory Beach! Did you have a reservation?"

"I'd like to speak to the owner, if that's possible," Vince replied.

"Um... of course! Let me just go find him. Back in a flash."

The server disappeared and reappeared with startling speed, trailed on his way back by a less enthusiastic man with a permanent scowl and a drooping face.

"Would it be possible to have a word in private?" Vince pressed, acutely aware of the queue that had formed behind him as he continued to occupy the entryway.

"Come on through, then," the owner drawled, turning and waddling towards the bar.

Vince glanced around and spotted three cameras in various corners of the room. He estimated there was one possible blind spot, behind a pillar leading to the kitchen, and did his best to subtly guide the manager towards it before taking his sunglasses and mask off.

"You wanted to talk to me? What's your name?" The man's accent couldn't have been any more stereotypical of a New Yorker.

"James Thomas. Pleasure to meet you." Vince extended a hand. "And you are?"

"Bobby Vegas. What did you want with me?"

"Do you have access to the apartments upstairs? I was hoping to get onto the roof."

Bobby folded his arms and raised an eyebrow. "Yeah, that's private property. I don't just let strangers walk in and go up there."

"What about paying customers?"

Vince reached into the pocket of his trench coat and subtly revealed a fifty-dollar bill.

"Gonna cost you more than that," Bobby replied nonchalantly.

Another fifty-dollar bill did nothing to alter the owner's unwavering stance before Vince finally gave in and pulled out a hundred to go alongside them.

"Alright. This way, please, sir."

Pulling on his mask and sunglasses, Vince followed Bobby through an unassuming door next to one labelled *Kitchen*. They continued up several flights of well-kempt stairs before eventually coming to a rusted metal door which gave way to the roof.

"I don't know you. You don't know me." Bobby took the words from Vince's mouth as they exchanged the money. "You want access again, it's the same price each time. Leave the money in an envelope at the bottom of the stairs as you pass through." He then disappeared back down the stairwell before Vince could say thanks.

The building atop which Vince stood only rose to just over half the height of the Sweeney Building. The windows of the top floor were still entirely inaccessible. What were accessible were the windows of flats on the fifth floor.

Vince inspected each of these in turn and found one of them to have been left open. He peered inside and didn't think he could see anyone, and so carefully lowered himself into what he determined to be the living room.

A quick survey of each room confirmed his initial suspicion that nobody was there and he proceeded quickly to the front door, using a spare key that he found in the kitchen to unlock it. First peering out before moving on into the hallway, he climbed the stairs until he reached the top floor.

Until that point, none of the landings had contained security cameras. That hadn't stopped Vince from checking every floor, though, and he was justified in his caution when he spotted the single security camera at the end of the corridor on the eleventh floor. He fished a small infrared laser pointer from his bag and aimed it at the camera's lens, just visible through the tinted glass of its encompassing dome. He then proceeded until he came upon the door marked *11B*.

A window at the end of the corridor could be opened without a key and Vince hoisted himself outside, precariously scaling the exterior windowsill. He shuffled along the ledge until he came upon a balcony, the layout of which he recognised from the flat's floorplan that he had found online.

The sliding door had been left unlocked and Vince gently pulled it open, just enough to squeeze through. He turned around and found himself face-to-face with a cat, its eyes narrowed with fierce suspicion.

Vince ignored the cat, pulling on a pair of latex gloves and setting to work. In every room he planted a camera, each not much larger than a pinhead and easily concealed amongst the assortment of various decorations and ornaments found all throughout the flat. These all contained microphones and fed directly to his phone, and he could also watch them through his neural chip.

Suitably satisfied that every square centimetre of Ellie Sunarav's flat was now under surveillance, he removed his gloves and exited the way he had come. Back out the balcony, scaling the walls, in through the window, down the stairs, through the flat on the fifth floor, out another window, down through the restaurant and back onto Main Street.

That wasn't all that needed to happen. Vince walked at a brisk pace to a locksmith two blocks away, uneasily fondling the key he had stolen from the flat on the fifth floor all the while.

A bell chimed as he opened the door and he breathed a sigh of relief to find he was the only customer there. A single man sat behind the counter and looked up, scoffing as he laid eyes upon Vince.

"You can take the mask off, kid. I've never worn 'em and I'm perfectly healthy."

Vince spotted a camera in the corner above the desk where the man sat and decided against following his advice. "I'm looking to get a key cut."

"Well, gee, I guess you're in the right spot, then," the man spoke with hefty sarcasm. "Let's see it, then."

Half an hour later and Vince found himself in possession of a duplicate key to flat 5A. On his way back to Main Street he stopped in at a dollar store—a term long since outdated—to buy a pack of envelopes. He placed two hundred dollars into one and dropped it at the bottom of the stairwell as he passed through the Ivory Beach on his way to the roof. Climbing back through the window into the flat, he strode to the kitchen to return the original key to exactly the place he had found it.

He hadn't accounted for a woman to be in there making her lunch.

"Don't scream, or I'll shoot you," Vince said coolly, caressing the handle of his pistol. "Understand?"

The woman's jaw hung open, her pupils dilated with fear as she failed to respond.

"Understand?" Vince repeated.

Finally, she gave a slight nod as she set down the knife she was using to butter a slice of bread.

"W-what do you want?" she stammered, shaking.

"Nothing to do with you. Do you live here alone?"

"I—Yes."

"Here's what's going to happen—I'm going to leave and you're going to pretend that this never happened. You're not going to report this to the police. You're not going to tell anybody that it happened. What you are going to do, however, is leave that window unlocked and open at all times. Are you following?"

She nodded.

"Should you transgress any of what I just said, I will come back and I will kill you. Is that understood?"

She nodded, and then stammered, "Y-yes."

"Good," Vince said. "Then I'm going to be leaving."

Walking backwards, Vince slipped a hand into his bag and attached one last camera to the underside of the kitchen counter before disappearing back through the window and onto the rooftop. He opened the door to the stairwell, checking over his shoulder to catch a glimpse of the woman staring at him through another window before flitting her eyes away. The first thing he did after stepping into the stairwell was unlock his phone.

The camera hadn't been placed with an especially useful view. The microphone, however, told him everything he needed to know.

"Hello? I need the police. A—a man with a gun just broke into my apartment. He threatened to kill me."

Vince sighed, unholstering his gun and switching off the safety.

CHAPTER 5

By the time the police had arrived, she was dead, and Vince was ten miles away.

The hitman didn't like to kill people unrelated to a job, but sometimes it had to happen. Especially in the case of those who chose to be uncooperative. The police weren't going to find any leads—he had scrubbed every last fingerprint. If they connected the dots with the window and the door on the roof, they would interview Bobby Vegas, who wouldn't have a lot to say. And a thousand dollars meant that the restaurant's security footage for that day had unfortunately been corrupted.

That's why Vince felt entirely at peace as he sat in front of the computer in Maddox's flat, idly watching the video feed from the cameras in flat 11B over several cups of tea.

It was only much later, in the evening, that someone finally appeared. It wasn't Ellie Sunarav but her husband, a man Vince knew to be Vimal Sunarav. He was an Indian businessman who fled the country after it was turned into a wasteland by Pakistani warheads. Despite the destruction of his assets in India, the conglomerate he had constructed still retained significant influence in North America and Europe.

The prostitute that came in with him wasn't much of a surprise, either, though Vince did feel compelled to mute the audio and look away for a while. The hitman eventually gave up on the idea that Ellie was going to make an appearance that evening and resigned to bed, having already fought against his circadian rhythm for several hours.

He watched the cameras for several hours in the morning after waking up, first witnessing the prostitute leave and then Vimal a couple hours later. Ellie never turned up and eventually Vince arranged to meet Hamzah at a café on 2nd Avenue on the Upper East Side.

Although they had arranged to meet for noon, Vince arrived at ten past and was disgruntled to find that he was still the first to arrive. A man matching Noah's description strolled in another five minutes later and sat down across from him, removing the sunglasses Vince noticed to be irritatingly similar to his own.

"Mr Foster." Hamzah proffered his hand, which Vince politely shook.

"Please, just Vince." He was certain he had already said that over the phone. "Noah speaks very highly of you."

"I am glad to hear that. I would speak highly of him in return. He is very good at what he does."

"That he is. More importantly, are you good at what you do?"

A waitress appeared and they both ordered medium black ersatz coffees, which Vince found unexplainably irritating.

"You do not need to worry about if I am good enough, Vince," Hamzah finally answered as the waitress departed. "I possess a skillset which means I have never made a mistake on a job. If you would like, I can provide you with contacts for previous employers, and they will speak more objectively than I would be able to."

"No, that's quite alright, I trust your word. Trust is key in our business, as I'm sure you know."

"Of course. This job could not exist without it."

Vince craned his neck in an attempt to spot any cars he thought could have been Hamzah's but only taxis lined the street outside. "Did you drive here?"

"No, I walked. I thought it would be more practical in a city such as New York."

"Maddox did give you a car, though?"

Hamzah nodded as the waitress reappeared with their drinks. He issued a quick word of gratitude, echoed awkwardly by Vince after she had already turned to walk away.

"What did you choose?" Vince pressed.

"I am not really a car person, so I was not fussed about having something nice. Just a Chevrolet SUV."

"A Chevy. You'll fit in here."

Vince unlocked his phone and navigated to documents pertaining to two particular individuals he had preselected as being suitable for Hamzah.

"As I said, I've got two targets and you get five million for the both of them. If you fuck either of them up, you don't get anything. Is that clear?"

Hamzah nodded attentively.

"We'll start with one and then go on to the next if you manage that." Vince opened a portrait of a woman—blonde hair, blue eyes, mid-thirties. "Introducing Jenna Fox. Chief engineer at New Orion. How does a trip to Phoenix sound?"

"It sounds long." Hamzah smirked, but Vince didn't reciprocate his mirth.

"These documents that Maddox provided are... sparse. You've got a lot of work cut out for you before you can actually strike. Jenna should be the easiest if only because of the fact that she isn't able to afford such a lavish life as the directors. Do you think you can do it?"

"Have no doubts, Vince. I will make you proud."

"The most difficult thing you'll encounter is the very strict boundary she maintains between her work and family life. You've got a husband and two kids to work around here. Can you manage that?"

"Please, Vince. I can do whatever it is you throw at me. Give me this chance and let me prove it to you. I will not let you down."

"Alright." Vince reluctantly sipped his coffee, unable to acclimate to the grainy, nutty taste of commonplace—and significantly cheaper—ersatz, and the pair sat in silence.

Hamzah was the first to finish his drink and he promptly stood up, shaking hands with Vince one more time before departing.

A notification on Vince's phone indicated that movement had been detected by one of the cameras in Ellie Sunarav's flat. His eyes were glued to the screen as he stood up and left the café, wandering semi-attentively in the direction of his car, parked in a multistorey block on 83rd Street.

She had finally made an appearance. Giving up on holding his phone as he struggled through the constant stream of pedestrians, Vince watched the surveillance through a stream generated by his neural chip. The first thing Ellie did after setting down her bag was grab a pre-brewed cup of coffee, genuine, from a machine on the kitchen counter. It was at that point that Vince realised he had notifications disabled for sudden spikes in audio.

Her routine then wasn't terribly interesting. She ordered a takeaway lunch which was delivered within twenty minutes before sitting down in front of the television to watch the news on MSNBC. After about twenty minutes, she turned it to some programme Vince didn't recognise on a streaming service. Thirty minutes later, the programme concluded and she left.

Later that evening, the cameras triggered another notification, though this time it was for the loud grinding of the coffee machine. Two minutes later, Ellie appeared and carried out much the same routine as had taken place at lunchtime. She was then joined some time later by Vimal, though they didn't engage in particularly extensive periods of interaction. Ellie retired to bed at ten o'clock, Vimal at half past eleven.

The same thing happened the following day. The same pre-brewed coffee, takeaway lunch, news, programme. The same almost identical routine in the evening. And it all happened again the day after that. Saturday and Sunday were different in that both Ellie and her husband spent more time at home, but the routine resumed from Monday and stayed mostly consistent for the next couple weeks.

On the Wednesday of the third week, Vince found himself on the roof of the Ivory Beach, clambering through the window of flat 5A on his way up to the eleventh floor. Ownership of the flat had passed from the woman Vince had killed to her parents, and the parents were yet to list the property on the market or attempt to find a tenant. As such, it remained empty.

The camera in the corridor on the eleventh floor didn't look to have been replaced and he was confident that it remained disabled. He climbed out of the window and scaled the wall around to the balcony before pressing his way inside. Ellie and Vimal never locked the back door. It was supposed to be inaccessible.

The grinding of the coffee machine began as Vince took position in the master bedroom, flattening himself against the wall between him and the living room.

The biometric lock to the front door clicked open with an accompanying beep and Ellie could be heard collecting the cup of coffee from the kitchen. Her heels clacked against the laminate floor as she made her way to sit on the sofa in front of the television. MSNBC blazed to life and she opened her phone to order her lunch, blissfully unaware of the hitman's presence no more than a metre behind her.

Vince waited. Fifteen minutes after Ellie's arrival, her lunch was delivered. A savoury aroma invigorated the air as she returned to the television. The news droned on. He wasn't listening to it. He was listening to her, each gentle stab of the fork, the muted chewing and swallowing, the scraping against the bottom of the container as she finished her lunch and set it to the side. She then opened Atmosphere, which Vince had learned was the name of the streaming service she used to watch her programme after the news. It was a subsidiary of Camden Space Corporation.

Emerging from behind the wall, he disabled her neural chip by tasering the side of her head. Only then did he unholster his pistol and point it at her head as he withdrew from his cover.

"Don't say a word, don't scream, don't attempt in any way to save yourself. If you ignore these instructions, I will pull this trigger without hesitation."

Ellie had been holding the cup of coffee when Vince had tasered her. It had spilled all over the cushions, which were white. He sighed and shook his head.

"What—" she attempted to say, but Vince cut her off.

"Don't say a word. Now stand up."

Ellie did as she was told, holding her hands by her head. Vince backed away, keeping his eyes unyieldingly trained on hers.

"Hands behind your head, fingers interlaced. Walk to the front door. Slowly."

She visibly trembled as she complied, Vince staying no more than a few steps behind her.

"You're going to walk down to the fifth floor. I'm putting my gun away, but be assured, I can draw it with more than enough time to kill you if you attempt to struggle. If we see anyone else, then we will walk past them. You will not show any sign of distress, you will not make eye contact. If you do, I will shoot you and the bystander. Open the door if you understand."

Ellie carefully removed one of her hands from behind her head to pull the door handle, pressing it gently and allowing momentum to swing it open.

"Good. Now walk."

Vince lowered his gun into his coat pocket as Ellie made a beeline for the stairwell, moving at a believable pace. He maintained a gap of two stairs, his hands in his pockets at all times.

Down and down they went, Ellie rigidly continuing to comply. At one point they passed someone, a resident, who didn't even so much as nod at them. Vince found himself thanking the ingrown abrasiveness of New Yorkers.

"Stop here." They came to the door marked 5 and Vince instructed Ellie to open it. She did, and that was when she chose to run.

The door slammed in Vince's face and in the precious seconds he spent opening it and running after her, she had already cried for help. Screaming at the top of her voice, it was impossible that nobody had heard her in the adjacent flats as he removed his gun from his pocket and knocked her over the head with it, stifling her screams as she fell unconscious. He swiftly unlocked the door to nearby flat 5A and hauled her into privacy just as the rattling of another lock sounded out across the corridor.

Vince closed the door just as a faint, "Hello?" was uttered. He dragged Ellie straight to the open window and launched her body onto the rooftop before climbing out himself and continuing to drag her over to the door leading to the restaurant stairwell.

The first police sirens arrived quickly. As Vince had predicted, they had found no leads pertaining to the killing of the woman who owned flat 5A. Unfortunately for him, that also meant they remained on high alert in the nearby vicinity. The resident on the fifth floor who had almost caught them must have called the police, and now Vince sat in the stairwell, on edge, administering Ellie with a lethal dose of cyanide by means of injection.

She died minutes later and the wailing of sirens rose to a crescendo as police vehicles flooded the street outside. Vince racked his brain for ideas, feeling very much like an ensnared animal of prey. The chuntering of a helicopter overheard ruled out any return to the roof. Leaving the corpse at the top of the stairs, Vince sauntered down towards the restaurant floor level to scope out any other possible exits. He passed a series of doors at each level, three in total, but he had no way of knowing what was behind them.

As he came to the ground floor, there was a marked heightening in the usual volume for the time of day. Vince opened the door and peeked out to see customers agitatedly chattering to themselves, the red-and-blue police lights streaming through and illuminating the restaurant interior like a disco.

He shut the door and bounded back up the stairs before running straight back down, this time lugging Ellie's body over his shoulder. He deposited it underneath the stairs on the ground floor before emerging into the restaurant and approaching Bobby Vegas, who was working behind the bar.

"Bobby," Vince said, smiling beneath his mask.

"Oh, James. You're a bit late today, aren't you?"

Vince had spent every lunchtime for the past four weeks at the Ivory Beach, always keeping his mask on until he had taken a seat at the only table where his face was out of view of the cameras. He did just this after a brief conversation with Bobby. Deliberating over a plate of lobster for an hour, he waited patiently, watching the livestream from the cameras in flat 11B over his neural chip. The police never entered it, and even if they had suspected anything, Vince knew they couldn't have broken down the door without a warrant. Eventually, they began to file back into their vehicles and drive away, entirely devoid of the urgency with which they had arrived.

"Did that have anything to do with you?" Bobby came to take Vince's plate as he stood up and donned his mask.

"You know I couldn't say, Bobby. There's another envelope waiting for you in the back, though. Oh, and if it's alright, I need to come back around closing time."

"What exactly are you up to? I'll tolerate you running
around on the roof but it better not be anything I get in
trouble for."

"If you don't speak to the police, then you don't get in
trouble. And you continue to make a lot of money. Let's
keep it that way, hm?"

When Vince returned to the Ivory Beach at midnight,
only drunks and homeless people occupied the streets.
The occasional police officer patrolled around to clear
them into the darker, less visible alleyways, but the average pedestrian was nowhere to be found. He parked his
car outside the restaurant's entrance, where Bobby waited
patiently, though he was also tangibly nervous.

"Look, I... I really think I ought to know what you're up
to," he stammered. "I'm not above taking a bribe for something petty, but if this is serious..."

Vince pulled an envelope out of his coat pocket and
held it in front of Bobby's face. "This envelope contains
five thousand dollars. I am going to give it to you and then
I am going to drive away and you will never see me again.
And if anyone asks about me, I was a tourist who took a
real liking to this place. Are the cameras rolling?"

Bobby glanced idly at a neon sign across the road before
answering. "Um... yes, they're rolling. They're always rolling. They're cameras, it's what they do."

"I'll need you to delete that footage."

Vince strode through the door into the restaurant, wedging it open, passing the bar and making his way straight to the stairway where he had left Ellie's body. Her muscles had stiffened under the first stages of rigor mortis and fitting her into a body bag wasn't an easy task in the enclosed space. When he did finally achieve it, he hauled the bag onto his shoulder and turned to leave the stairwell.

Through the window, he spotted Bobby with his phone to his ear. He dropped the body bag and retrieved his infrared laser, disabling all the cameras before falling prone and crawling towards the entrance.

"...yeah, he's out back." Vince listened to Bobby's conversation through the open door. "I can't see him, so I dunno what he's getting up to. Some shady stuff, man, I ain't got a good feeling about it. He's not gonna be long, I don't think, so... send some people over, fast. He's dangerous, alright?"

The fear permeating Bobby's voice was exacerbated by Vince's sudden appearance as he pressed himself up from the floor and cocked his gun. He hadn't ended the call, and Vince could see the numbers *911* clearly across the top of the screen.

"Hang up," he mouthed, momentarily pulling his mask down.

As soon as Bobby hung up, Vince shot him in the head.

CHAPTER 6

For the second time that day, Vince found himself overwhelmed by sirens. Except this time, they knew that he
was their target.

After killing Bobby, Vince acted very quickly. He
sprinted into the restaurant and lugged Ellie's bagged
corpse out onto the street and into the boot of his car before practically diving into the driver's seat and starting the
engine. That was when the first police car arrived. Its sirens roared to life as the officers inside spotted Bobby's
mutilated body while Vince slammed on the accelerator
and raced away.

As he weaved through the New York nightlife traffic, he
found himself again blessing his choice in the Corolla. Although humble, it remained extraordinarily manoeuvrable

through the windy Brooklyn Streets. Not enough to lose the police so quickly, though.

A second vehicle blazed onto the scene and Vince swerved to avoid it, almost crashing into a parked digger. He turned onto a straight and put his foot down, being thrown back in his seat by the sheer force of acceleration.

"NYPD! Stop the vehicle!" the megaphone from one of the pursuing cars boomed.

Taxi horns blared as Vince sped past, switching frequently to the left-hand side of the road to overtake, before turning onto a one-way road in the wrong direction. A van flashed its lights and its horn boomed, forcing Vince to detour onto the pavement where he dodged a small tree and squeezed through a gap between a metal fence and several parked cars before returning to the road. The police were no longer behind him, but their sirens still penetrated the night air.

The whirling of blades indicated they had been reinforced by a helicopter and Vince scrambled to avoid its searchlight with pure speed owing to the lack of overhead cover. He made his way out of the network of narrow streets back onto a two-way street, where he accelerated even faster in the search for cover. He passed under a bridge which had no place to stop and raced ahead, back towards the Sweeney Building and the adjacent Manhattan Bridge.

The road widened on approach to the bridge and Vince made a sudden handbrake turn to land on an even bigger street with a central reservation. He didn't spend long there, turning quickly right and zooming ahead to the underpass. A car park directly in its centre was mostly empty and Vince swerved into a spot between two other cars, turning off the engine and killing the lights.

The searchlight continued to illuminate patches of the nearby area and the sirens continued to wail. He removed his sunglasses and mask before stepping out of the car and hailing a passing taxi.

"Upper West Side, please," he said curtly. The taxi driver nodded wordlessly and rolled away, merging onto the Brooklyn Bridge and carrying on towards the block of flats in which Vince was staying.

The garage door opened automatically as he strolled up to its entrance and he was greeted by the same android that had given him the first set of keys. This time, he opted for the SUV, a BMW iX6.

On his way back to the underpass he stopped at a recharge station and bought several containers of lighter fluid and a lighter. The cashier gave him a strange look as he paid, which could have also been in part due to his sunglasses.

The police were still searching for Vince by the time he arrived back to the underpass and he acted rapidly to transfer the body bag from the Corolla to the iX6. He then scrubbed the dashboard and steering wheel of any fingerprints before dousing every part of the car in the lighter fluid to an amused crowd of homeless people.

The underpass bathed in bright yellow light as the Corolla burst into flame with Vince's departure. He drove casually into the night, passing police cars racing to the scene of the bonfire. Returning to the flats, he parked the car back in the garage and headed up for the night.

The following morning, Vince drove back to the Sweeney Building after Vimal had left for the day. From his surveillance he had gathered that Ellie's husband was not in the slightest way concerned with her absence and had gone about his business as usual. Helpfully, he hadn't reported her as missing, with the extent of his concern expressed with, "That woman," upon seeing the coffee stains on the sofa.

It took Vince all of three seconds from rounding the corner onto Water Street, the location of the Ivory Beach, to spot the stakeout vehicle. It was parked on the road outside a block of modern flats two buildings over from the restaurant, with a clear view of the location where he had killed Bobby. The area was by no means clear, with swarms of pedestrians milling between the myriad shopping outlets and other restaurants in the popular tourist spot.

Vince cursed and carried on driving past the van, the two officers inside not even attempting to be subtle with their surveillance. In any other situation, he would have given up for the day and waited for another time after the police had given up. But with a decomposing body in the back of his car, he had no choice but to act before anyone realised she was missing.

He took a right further up the road into a little car park and came to a stop in one of the few empty spaces. He had to assume that the police had an idea of his appearance and he left his trench coat in the car before strolling out into the main thoroughfare. Still remaining were his mask and glasses, which he refused to give up despite the fact that the police wouldn't have known his face without them. He didn't look out of place—it was a sunny day and plenty of residents and tourists alike wore pollution masks. What he didn't trust, though, was the idea that a person of his description entering the seafood restaurant wouldn't arouse suspicion.

Instead of the seafood restaurant, he tried one building over, a pharmacy adjacent to the block of flats in front of which the police had parked. A wary glance at the van revealed that they hadn't even watched him go in, their eyes lazily tunnel-visioned on the entrance to the Ivory Beach.

Several customers already occupied the store, idly browsing products that Vince thought utterly out of place in a pharmacy. He made his way straight to the counter and straightened his posture, speaking plainly and confidently.

"Hi, I need to get onto the roof. Can you let me up?"

The cashier, flustered, initially struggled for words before spitting out, "I—uh, I don't—"

"I'm here for the maintenance works."

"Oh! I guess? I didn't know we had maintenance works."

"I've been booked in for this morning. I am on the clock, though, so I'd appreciate it if we hurried."

The cashier looked frantically at various things Vince couldn't see behind the counter before finally nodding and producing a set of keys. She beckoned him to the door behind the counter and inserted the keys.

"I like your accent. Are you from England?"

"London. But I've lived here a while."

The lock clicked open and the cashier held the door open for Vince, who nodded in appreciation.

"Wait—do you have any ID? I should probably just check that so I don't get in trouble with my manager."

He set his bag down and rifled around for his wallet, finding it and selecting one of several identification cards.

"Next time you see them, just let them know I'm up on the roof. I might even be finished before that happens."

Satisfied with her inspection of Vince's ID, the cashier allowed him through, and he nodded one final time before proceeding upstairs.

He wasted no time in flying up the stairs and bursting through the door at the top. The building wasn't quite as tall as the restaurant, and the next roof over was out of reach. It was possible, however, to climb onto a ledge lining the front of the flats above the restaurant. But that would mean exposing himself to the stream of people below.

Anxious pacing around the roof produced no other solutions. The air conditioning units and fans noisily chuntering away were positioned too far from the wall. The backside of the building was a sheer drop. As much as Vince hated the risk, he was left with no other option.

His eyes fell upon the stakeout van as he swung onto the front ledge and the police were quick to spot him. They both rushed out of the vehicle and tore into the restaurant as Vince pulled himself onto the higher roof and raced towards the window to flat 5A.

Reinforcements in the form of sirens cut through the air almost immediately as he dived into the flat and scrambled towards the door. He balanced subtlety with urgency once he made his way into the corridor and began to climb the stairs to the top floor.

The police had reached the roof of the Ivory Beach by the time Vince reached the window on the eleventh floor. He waited for them to proceed into the building before clambering out and scaling around onto the balcony. More police had arrived, cars flooding the street below, by the time he had reached said balcony.

What ensued was a mentally rehearsed retrieval of every single camera stationed throughout the Sunaravs' flat. In a series of practised movements, Vince strode from room to room until a final check on the video feed confirmed every last device had been disabled and collected.

That was when his next move became difficult. While inside Ellie's flat, he knew he was safe. The police couldn't have suspected he was there. But he was also unable to leave.

So began the waiting game. For hours Vince stayed motionless in a storage cupboard, the most secluded place he could find and completely out of view of the windows. Every now and then he stepped outside to survey the street below, finding the police still to be present a couple hours later. But their numbers slowly dwindled until finally, several hours later, Vince found the confidence to emerge from the flat.

As he had now done so many times, he left the way he had come in. All his equipment recuperated, the job done, he was almost home free. Once he reached the roof, he opted to leave via the stairs in the pharmacy, finding the door at the bottom of the stairs to be locked. He raised his hand to knock but then hesitated, instead bringing his ear to the door to listen to the muffled conversation taking place behind the counter.

"...comes along and lies to her. I didn't book no maintenance guy today. I don't manage the building, for Christ's sake. And I called the landlord and he said what I was thinking—there's no maintenance guy booked. I don't know who this guy is, but he's up there and he shouldn't be."

Vince retreated slowly back up the stairs until he came to the door for the flat on the first floor. It would have taken too long to pick the lock, so instead he resorted to brute force.

One kick was enough to alert the officer behind the counter to his presence, and two kicks were enough to break down the door. He ran through the flat, the officer's calls echoing behind him. It was impossible to hide with the light pouring through the window, but Vince tried anyways as he ducked behind the counter separating the kitchen from the living room.

"Come out with your hands in the air," the officer decreed, his radio abuzz with activity. Vince heard only one set of footsteps and caressed the handle of his taser as he waited patiently for the officer to move closer.

He launched into the air and grabbed the officer's gun before bringing the taser to his head. After frying his neural chip, Vince punched him around the head to knock him unconscious before heading straight to the window, opening it and jumping out.

The walk back to his car was liberatingly calm. It was a long drive to D.C. and Vince only stopped twice. The first time was at a service station to grab something to eat and to refuel the car. The second was to take a detour off the interstate into the forests of New Jersey to bury Ellie's body.

CHAPTER 7

Hamzah arrived in Phoenix two days after his meeting with Vince, having travelled leisurely by car, resting overnight in a motel. Any downtime was spent researching, though publicly accessible information about Jenna Fox was sparse.

He was able to vindicate Vince's claim as to the composition of her family. Her social media accounts were private, but the few images that were available clearly depicted herself with a man and two children.

For the money that she was making, though not quite as much as a director, she lived remarkably humbly. A bungalow in a northern suburb utterly homogeneous amongst the sea of others just like it. Her husband drove a black Chevrolet pickup, and she a Buick SUV in silver. On the latter car Hamzah planted a tracker after following her to the supermarket after work one day.

Although he had assured Vince of his capability, Hamzah felt somewhat out of his depth in the scale of the challenge. He might have been a proficient hitman, but he had never made anyone disappear. There had always been evidence, so much of his time in the city was spent researching.

When he wasn't researching, he was tailing or staking out. He spent a lot of time parked on the street outside the Fox household, feeling somewhat conspicuous at times. But his tinted windows meant that nobody could see him inside the vehicle, at least. Nor could they hear him as he recorded voice notes to review later.

"Jenna's husband doesn't work," he monologued. "He is a homemaker. Very rare in the post-war West, but Jenna makes enough money to make it work. Unfortunately it also means that I will not be able to strike at the home. I must find somewhere else."

His opportunity came in the form of a book club. Every Wednesday, after work, Jenna drove to a library in neighbouring Scottsdale where she spent two hours with a group of seven others. Hamzah spent several weeks staking this out, too, and Jenna was always, without fail, the first to leave.

It was one of these weeks at around six-thirty in the evening that he received a tap on his window during a stakeout. He cautiously fondled his gun in his pocket and lowered the window just a crack to view the person that had approached him in more clarity. It was a woman, short blonde hair not unsimilar to Jenna. She was much younger, though—Hamzah would have guessed twenty-five.

"Can I help you?" he asked unassumingly.

"Could you please lower the window more?" Her accent was incomprehensibly thick, some variety of French. "I'd like to talk to you."

"I'm sorry, I am not interested."

She twitched her hand to reveal the barrel of a pistol, holding it discreetly beneath the flap of her jacket and pointing it at Hamzah.

"It wasn't a request."

His eyes widened and he pressed the button to let the window fall completely open.

"Give me your weapon."

He tried to send a message to Noah via his neural chip but was met with only error messages reading *Unable to deliver*.

"Don't make this messy."

"Okay," Hamzah agreed, panicking as he tried and failed a final time to reach out to Noah. He slowly raised the gun he had been clenching in his pocket and rotated it to hand it hilt-first to his assailant.

"I am going to get into the back seat of the car and you are going to drive where I tell you. If you try anything, I will shoot you. Do you understand?"

"Yes."

She opened the door and moved into the back seat like a fluid, the barrel of her gun trained constantly on Hamzah's head.

"Go."

They drove for an hour out into the desert, Hamzah's mind alight all the while with calculation as to finding a way out of his situation. He found a chance in the form of an oncoming pickup truck.

He had a window of maybe half a second in which he could lurch the car out over in front of the oncoming vehicle without allowing his kidnapper time to readjust herself and shoot him, while also ensuring the truck crashed into them. He executed it perfectly.

They had been travelling at about seventy miles per hour and it was a formidable matchup. Both cars spiralled out of control onto the side of the road, the SUV containing Hamzah and his abductor rolling with the momentum. He absorbed much of the force owing to his seatbelt—his abductor wasn't afforded the same luck as she was tossed about the back seat like a ragdoll.

When they finally came to a stop, the car leaning and settling upside down, Hamzah unbuckled and scurried to escape through the smashed windscreen. Two shots rang out from behind him, bullets whizzing past his head as he found solid ground. He began to run towards the ruined pickup, its owner angrily but confusedly twisting himself out of the driver's seat.

"What in God's name did you think you were doing?" he yelled. "Do you know what speed that was?"

Another shot cracked through the air and the crashed pickup was then decorated with the man's blood and brains as Hamzah's abductor emerged, bleeding and bruised, from the wreckage of the SUV.

"Stop right there," she seethed, her barrel again pointed at Hamzah's head. He cast a weary glance across the corpse of the man before falling to his knees in defeat and meeting the woman's cold gaze.

She came to stand beside him and tasered his head, erasing any lingering hopes that he might have been able to get a message to someone. His stomach felt hollow as she then proceeded to reveal a device he could only have guessed was a radio frequency jammer, tossing it to the side in disgust. The crash had damaged it beyond repair.

Two bullets tore through Hamzah's legs and he screamed through gritted teeth. His assailant knocked him backwards and his arms sprawled out to his sides, where two more bullets mangled each of his hands. Vomit surged to the back of his throat and he turned his head to spew over the bloodstained ground as she fell upon him, placing a knee onto his chest.

"Who are you working for?"

Hamzah swished saliva around his mouth and turned his head to the other side to spit. As he turned back to face his abductor, he was struck hard enough to force tears to well in his eye.

"Who are you working for?"

"Why would I tell you? You are just going to kill me anyways."

"You don't know who I am. You don't have neural footage of me. There's no DNA evidence to trace me. If you give me what I want, then I will let you go."

What Hamzah faced was a traditional question of honour over life. Was he willing to betray Vince to stay alive?

It wouldn't have been very honourable. But in the post-war world, honour was very much a dead construct. All the remained was survival of the fittest.

"Vince Foster." He didn't feel comfortable as the words left his mouth.

"And where can I find Vince Foster?"

"I last met with him in New York. I do not know where he has gone from there."

The pressure was relieved from his chest as she stood up and nodded.

"Thank you."

The ringing of the gunshot was only a wisp in the howling of the evening wind.

CHAPTER 8

The penthouse Maddox owned in D.C. managed to make the New York flat look cheap. It was several times larger, with private facilities ranging from a gym to a spa. It had a view of Capitol Hill over the Anacostia River and a private helicopter pad next to the heated outdoor pool on the roof. It was here that Vince allowed himself one day of relaxation before he began to work on his next target.

He was mostly unsatisfied with the job in New York. It had been messy. And it was a miracle that he had managed to distance himself from Ellie's disappearance, with a recent news story describing how she had finally been registered as missing. His second target would be easier, though, as he lived in a Virginia suburb away from the throb of civilisation. Fewer people, fewer cameras, fewer police. He looked forward to it.

His target's name was Spencer Fitzpatrick. He was the youngest member of the board at only twenty-seven years old. This could probably have been attributed to the fact that his father was also on the board. Being assigned a target as young as Spencer was always exciting for Vince, as they usually hadn't had the chance to build themselves much of a life. It was easier to make them disappear. And with Spencer living alone in a thirty-million-dollar house, there was more than enough opportunity.

Vince woke up early the day after his break and drove along the Potomac River under cover of darkness towards 1165 Chain Bridge Road. He spent the rest of the day in the car, scouting out the neighbourhood in the morning and staking out the house in the afternoon.

The next day was much the same. He began to learn Spencer's routine and discovered that, despite his romantic solitude, he was prone to bringing home female guests. That wasn't an obstacle Vince was worried about—he preferred it to wives and girlfriends. He was more worried about the network of CCTV cameras covering the entire driveway and surrounding road.

Publicly accessible data about the property revealed it had an expansive garden which extended as far as the border to the nearby main road, Dolley Madison Boulevard. On another day, after watching Spencer leave, Vince pulled over at the side of the road and traversed his way through the entangling foliage separating the suburb from the road. The only barricade beyond that was a meagre fence erected around the garden's edges for decorative purposes. He vaulted this without issue and continued on past the swimming pool and towards the house.

He slipped on a pair of gloves before trying the back door and finding it, as expected, to be locked. Undeterred, he retrieved a set of lockpicks from his bag and spent five minutes setting the pins before twisting the handle and successfully allowing himself access to the house.

As with the Sunaravs' flat, Vince set about rigging every single room with cameras. It took a while longer, but eventually it was done, and he decided he would head back to the penthouse for the day.

He had just reached the car when the click of the gun froze him in place, and he didn't dare to so much as twitch a muscle. He felt its cold barrel press against the back of his head as his assailant spoke.

"Vince Foster." A woman, distinguishably Parisian accent. "You're going to get into the car and I am going to sit in the back seat and you are going to drive where I tell you."

Vince quickly sent a message to Maria via his neural chip as a sharp pang of pain shot through his skull with its ejection. Pocketing it and stepping away, she stepped around to finally come into the hitman's view—short blonde hair, dressed modestly in a white button-up blouse, black faux leather trousers, tinted sunglasses concealing her eyes. Her face was cold, deadly serious. It was also bedecked with fresh scars.

"Who sent you?" Vince asked.

"You don't get to ask questions. Get in the car."

He did as instructed and slowly grasped the handle to the car door, sliding into the driver's seat in perfect synchrony with the Parisian's descent into the back, her gun ever pointed at his skull.

"You're Eurint, then? Or has someone hired you?"

His abductor remained silent as Vince started the car and rolled onto the boulevard.

"A name then. You know mine, give me yours. Or at least a fake one. Something I can address you with."

"Mr Foster, you are a professional. So am I. Please treat me as such."

Vince quietly accepted his defeat in the moment and remained silent as he drove on. After removing his gun from his pocket, the Parisian spoke only to give directions, and those directions were brief.

"Turn left."

"Turn right."

"I need the toilet. Can we stop at the services?" That was Vince.

"No."

Several hours later and a couple hundred miles along the interstate, it was the car that needed servicing rather than him. "We keep going much longer and we're going to run out of charge."

"Take this exit."

Vince signalled and turned off as instructed, landing upon a lonely country road passing several fast-food restaurants and a recharge station. Despite the needle's ominous loitering in the red, he was not told to turn in and instead carried on down the road.

"Turn left."

Vince hadn't expected the instruction and brought the car to a sharp halt as he made his way onto a driveway already housing two cars. Next to the driveway was an old bungalow, wood showing signs of decay and the patio outside the front door worn thin from decades of use. A postbox sat uprooted at the end of the drive, unused.

"Get out of the car."

"If this is just an execution site, might I suggest somewhere more secluded?" He was biding his time.

"Get out of the car."

Vince unbuckled and exited the car, stretching and backing a safe distance away as the Parisian did the same. She used her gun to gesture him towards the house and he walked slowly to the front door, warily traversing the dilapidated stairs and patio. He grasped the doorknob, finding it to be loose but managing to open the door.

A pervasive musk infiltrated his nose and forced him to recoil as hazy yellow lights flickered on. The blinds on the windows were shut and the differing colours on opposing sides implied that they had been for some time. The Parisian urged him to take a seat on a raggedy sofa which must have been almost a hundred years old, judging by its unsavoury physical state and the little knowledge Vince had of historical furniture design.

A television, not as old as the furniture, switched on as the Parisian found a remote control and turned the channel to some arbitrary news. Vince wasn't focused on that—his mind was racing as to how he could escape. He was counting on his message to Maria bringing help, but whether it would come in time, he didn't know.

His abductor dragged a wooden chair from across the room and placed it to sit in front of Vince, crossing her legs and resting her gun on her lap.

"Who are you working for, Vince?"

That surprised him. He had been certain from the moment of abduction that he had been betrayed. If that wasn't the case, then he figured he still had a way out without being killed.

"You're a professional. So am I. Please treat me as such."

Her blow was sharp and hard, Vince gritting his teeth as he brought a hand to his cheek.

"Who are you working for?"

"In what scenario did you think I would freely divulge information like that? Would you?"

A second blow came with even more strength than the first, leaving his other cheek feeling raw. He stayed defiant, reclining in his chair and straightening his hair.

"Unlock your phone."

"Not on your life."

"Unlock it or I will saw off your head and unlock it myself."

"Don't be crude. You know full well I can brick that phone with one command."

The Parisian scowled and stood up, cocking her gun and placing its barrel against Vince's forehead. He stared straight into her eyes, maintaining an entirely neutral expression.

"Vince, my employer is not so interested in keeping you alive. This whole routine here is a preventative measure, to stop your employer from sending out any more assassins. But I have express permission to kill you if you do not cooperate. That way, the murders still stop, even if we do not find out who ordered them."

"You're going to kill me already? Before even attempting torture? For a professional, that's really quite amateur."

The butt of her gun collided with Vince's temple and he fell onto his side, grunting and rubbing the site of impact. She disappeared, only briefly, returning with a briefcase which opened to reveal a wicked set of torture implements.

Hurry up, Maria, Vince thought as the Parisian bound his hands to separate legs of a table she hauled over from across the room.

"Where should we start, Vince? Are you right-handed or left-handed? Or I could just break all the fingers on both. That would make driving difficult, I should think. And shooting."

"It would be more painful to rip off my fingernails."

That's exactly what she did. One by one, Vince was deprived of his fingernails, fiercely suppressing the pained howls that yearned to escape. Each passing minute felt like a lifetime and the Parisian only became more and more enraged by his continued refusal to speak.

After that it was tasering. Ten-second bursts between the same, repeated question, Vince always finding the resolve to refuse to answer.

"Who are you working for?"

A shadow passed by the window behind the Parisian and Vince raised his hands in feigned surrender.

"Okay," he spluttered, spitting out blood that had pooled in his mouth from sustained beating. His eye was swollen and his hair was a dishevelled mess, his head was rocked by a throbbing headache and his lip was split. "I'll tell you."

"Don't mess around with me, Vince. You will regret it."

The SWAT team kicked down the door and distracted the Parisian for long enough to allow Vince to kick her legs, toppling her off-balance as she found herself the target of several automatic rifle barrels.

"Don't kill her!" Vince shrilled. One of the agents kneeled down to free him while another removed her neural chip. The hitman went straight to the bathroom to clean up his wounds before reappearing and leaning down to whisper aggressively into the Parisian's ear.

"I won't press charges, but I never want to see you again." He then retrieved both guns and his own neural chip before standing back up.

"Thank you," he nodded at the team of officers that had overwhelmed the room before letting his eyes fall contemptuously to the isolated hitwoman.

After reinserting and readapting to his chip, Vince found a message from Maria reading only *SWAT on their way*. He had sent her the SUV's registration plate upon his assault and that had been more than enough for her to enable the police to track him. It also meant that he would have to ditch the car.

The Parisian was handcuffed and escorted out into the back of one of the BearCats waiting outside. Vince himself was escorted into the back of a Cadillac with two other officers and they turned back around to head onto the eastbound interstate.

"So who are you?" one of the officers asked.

"No comment," Vince said nonchalantly.

"Did you know her?"

"No comment."

A twenty-minute drive landed the convoy in the town of Staunton. The cars all pulled into the parking bay at the police station and Vince was shown into another vehicle which took him to the local hospital while the Parisian was escorted unceremoniously into the station.

It was late in the evening by the time he returned, bandages binding all of his fingers together like mittens. The police were eager to finally speak to him, having spent hours interrogating their prisoner. From what Vince had gathered, she hadn't said a whole lot.

"I don't want to press charges."

The reaction was furore. The police tried to convince him to change his mind, but it was in vain. The night ended with Vince being driven back to the site of the torture where he returned to the BMW and set off back to D.C., visiting another of Maddox's garages and exchanging the SUV for a more low-profile Ford F-150. Low-profile of course referring to its popularity, rather than its size. It was a monstrous vehicle.

It didn't look at all out of place in the underground car park of the flat block in downtown D.C., which was where it would stay until the night that Vince made his move. He couldn't risk another vehicle being identified now that he knew he was being followed. The Parisian couldn't have been the last.

Even though Vince didn't want to press charges, the prosecutor did anyways. Under the name Celine Lavalette, the invalidity of which he didn't doubt for a second, his assailant was charged with felony kidnapping and torture. She was granted bail, but at a cost of one million dollars owing to the severity of the offences. It was posted within a week and she disappeared.

Vince looked up the identity of the person recorded as having paid the money. They didn't exist.

CHAPTER 9

Eight weeks passed and Vince spent most of it in the penthouse, ensuring the windows remained permanently opaque. He had essentials delivered and left outside the front door, sending the android to then inspect the contents of any bags. Unlike in the New York flat, this android came with the option to be muted, which made Vince very content.

Eight weeks was a long time for what he deemed to be the easiest of his targets. But he wanted to make sure it was clean and he wanted time to throw off any pursuers. He had long since learned Spencer's routine. He woke up no earlier than ten o'clock on weekdays, noon on weekends. He then drove to his office in D.C. before coming home at about nine, though this varied depending on whether he went out drinking after his evening meal. Vince calculated that he brought a girl back on fifty per-cent of non-drinking weekdays, rising to eighty-five per-cent when he drank. Then he would go to bed in the late hours, no matter whether he had a companion or not.

The girls he brought home always stole from him. He would leave them alone in the house whenever he went to work in the morning, and it would be some stray cash or an expensive ornament or an item of designer clothing. He always noticed whenever he came home, but he didn't seem to care.

His weekends were spent moping around. Every single week, without fail, Vince would spend both Saturday and Sunday watching Spencer lounge around his house, milling from room to room to unenthusiastically watch television or play video games or emulate drugs. He would order food and his brief exchange of words with the delivery driver seemed to be the happiest period of the day, right before sinking back into apathy.

When Vince parked on the edge of Dolley Madison Boulevard, he waited in the car for an hour before step-ping out. He used an application in his neural chip to rec-ord the registration plate of every single car that passed by. When none of them ever pinged up as a duplicate, he felt confident enough to press on.

It was Sunday evening and Spencer remained lethargic as ever. His dinner had long since been delivered and eaten. Vince trudged up through the back garden, grabbing the back door handle and shaking it vigorously before re-treating around one of the wooden posts holding up the roof of the veranda. The noise was enough to coax Spencer to investigate, and he was in no way prepared to react to Vince emerging and tasering him in the head.

The hitman knocked him unconscious with a precise blow to the temple and administered cyanide in the same way he had done with Ellie. The body was bagged and transferred to the back of the pickup truck and Vince went back into the house to remove all the cameras.

He drove away, heading west along the I-66. He buried the body fifteen hundred miles away in the desert west of Austin, Texas.

CHAPTER 10

Vince chose a restaurant on the eightieth floor of the McCarthy Tower not because of its opulence but because it was the only place he felt certain he wasn't being followed. It also offered a prime view of the city, which had almost doubled in size since pre-war times.

John McCarthy was one of the many London oligarchs that had seized control of the power and wealth vacuum presented by the city's declaration of independence in the wake of the war. He was a close ally of Oliver Maddox, and despite being a London oligarch spent most of his time in the States.

Noah arrived exactly on time as the sun set over the distant Lake Travis and it was immediately clear from his expression that something was amiss. Vince waited until the waiter, an android, had ordered their drinks before asking about it.

"Are you going to tell me what that expression's about?"

Noah took a deep breath. "I've lost contact with Hamzah."

"What?" Vince tried to send a message via his neural chip and was met with an error. "Noah, if he—"

"I don't know what happened to him. But we can make it work."

"When did you notice? Why didn't you tell me?"

A period of silence ensued as the android returned with their drinks and then asked for their mains, but Vince hadn't even looked at the menu. They instructed it to come back later.

"I didn't tell you because I didn't want you to panic. Like you're doing now."

"I think he might have spilled. I was attacked, Noah." He removed his mutilated hands from beneath the table where he had been concealing them and Noah recoiled in disgust. "She ambushed me. I hadn't even spotted her. And she knew exactly where to find me. We had a leak."

"But he wouldn't... I don't see why..."

"I trusted him too quickly. I should never have done it. The whole job is in jeopardy now."

"Wait, Vince, wait. You're being irrational. Let's start at the beginning—how did she know to follow Hamzah?"

Vince took a deep breath of his own and sipped from his drink, a genuine black coffee.

"I don't know. I didn't get a chance to interrogate her personally. I messaged Maria and she sent in a SWAT team to arrest her. Whoever she was, she didn't talk to the police, and she fled before she could be convicted."

"Where?"

"Europe, I imagine. She was French. Didn't bother masking her accent. And I don't know about you, but I don't see any reason for European agents to interfere with assassination attempts on New Orion directors. If anything, I would have thought they'd encourage it."

"I would agree." Noah glanced askance at the android as it made its way back towards them.

This time, they did order their mains—Vince a marinated ribeye steak, Noah grilled scallops with creamed corn.

"Have you taken out any of your targets?" Vince asked quietly.

"L.A. is done. I landed in Sacramento last week and have spent the time since researching."

"I've done two out of my three. Did Hamzah hit any of his?"

Noah shook his head sheepishly.

"That's one more each, then. I'll take Salt Lake City, you can have Phoenix. But before any of that happens, we're finding out who this woman is, and who she's working for."

The conversation assumed a much lighter tone from that point onwards and their meals arrived in rapid fashion. They ate in relative silence, amplified by the fact that they were the only diners in the entire restaurant. Vince could understand why—the prices were four times what he would have expected to pay at a normal location, and

McCarthy Tower wasn't open to just anybody. They were only allowed in owing to their connection to Maddox.

As such, it came as a surprise when a cohort of FBI agents strolled through the entryway from the corridor, eyes dead set on Vince and Noah as they finished off their mains. The pair of hitmen shared a wary glance as they were suddenly surrounded.

"Vince Foster. Noah Cox," one of the agents, a grey-haired man of imposing height, spoke. "Finley Clarke, FBI. I'll need you to come with me."

"Can we ask what this is about?"

"You may not. Please follow me."

"Are we under arrest?"

"Not at present. Please allow us to keep it that way."

Vince and Noah glanced at each other again before counting out enough cash to cover the cost of the meal and leaving it on the table as they were led away by the agents.

They filed neatly into the lift and plummeted down to the bottom floor, being shown directly to the car park where several Chevrolet SUVs awaited. They drove half an hour into the northern region of the city, where the old FBI offices were situated. Developmentally, these build-ings had fallen far behind the rest of the city, a beige eye-sore amongst the modern glass-walled high-rises.

"Gonna need you both to remove your chips, please."

"I don't know—" Vince tried to protest.

"It's standard procedure. Nobody's allowed them on site. Any phones, you'll have to leave them in the foyer, too."

Although the site's exterior was in need of a facelift, the interior was the exemplification of modernity. Sharp geometry, clean white surfaces and minimalism reminiscent of the twenties, screens flush with the walls to the point where it was impossible to spot the seams. An android stood behind the reception desk and exchanged Vince and Noah's phones and neural chips for a pair of marked tokens. The pair were then led through security, where they were also relieved of their guns and tasers.

Once they were past security, they were escorted under close watch by the agents that had accompanied them the entire journey. The FBI facility continued to radiate modernity as they passed rooms not unsimilar to police interrogation chambers and offices full of forward-facing technicians and analysts tapping fervently away before computer screens.

They turned into a nearby lift where the agents issued a command to take them to the third floor. A short jaunt through more open-plan offices led them to a section of meeting rooms and closed-off individual offices. The agents ushered them separately into two of these rooms, the opaque windows preventing vision of the interiors.

"Please, Mr Foster, take a seat." Vince was greeted inside the chamber by another agent, a middle-aged woman, who gestured towards the chair facing the window on one side of a small grey table. A link protruded from the table's surface which Vince assumed was for the purpose of restraint, though he was not handcuffed. She then proceeded to take the seat across from him while he looked contemptuously at the window's hazy surface.

"Mr Foster," the agent began. "What's your purpose for being in the United States?"

"Am I under arrest?" Vince repeated stubbornly.

"No, Mr Foster. We'd just like to ask you some questions."

"Which I don't have to answer."

"We would really prefer it if you do. Please—"

"Am I allowed to have a lawyer present?"

"Mr Foster, do you really want to get a lawyer involved? All we're asking for here is a little bit of cooperation. You help us, and we won't have to arrest you. What's your purpose for being in the United States?"

Vince sighed. "Work."

"And you have a valid visa?"

"Is that a joke?"

"What do you do for a living, Mr Foster?"

"Freelance security consulting."

"Who are you working for right now?"

"That's private information. My clients appreciate being kept secret to ensure that my work remains uninfluenced by figures within their organisations."

The agent raised her eyebrows, her gaze focused on a tablet on the table in front of her. Vince tried to look at the device, but its contents were obfuscated from his point of view by a privacy screen. "Okay, let's move on. What's your relationship to Ellie Sunarav?"

"Never heard of her." His expression was unwavering.

"What about Khanna McNeill?"

He didn't bother to respond orally this time, instead only obstinately shaking his head. He did the same when she asked, "And Spencer Fitzpatrick?"

"You were recently in New York City." The agent had become terse, dropping the friendly act upon accepting her inability to overcome Vince's aversion. "What was the purpose of your visit?"

"Work."

"For this... unspecified company? Or is it an individual?"

"No comment. Agent, I would appreciate an explanation as to why I was escorted from my meal."

She took a deep breath before paging through her tablet. "Mr Foster, you've been named as a person of interest in the case of the disappearance of three directors from the board of New Orion, the space exploration and moon mining firm. I'm sure you know of it?"

He nodded.

"CCTV footage has been handed over to the FBI showing footage of a person with your likeness in and around New York City on the date of and leading up to Ellie Sunarav's disappearance. The same goes for Washington and Spencer Fitzpatrick, while your colleague in the other room has been spotted in L.A."

"Him or someone with his likeness, as you put it?"

"The identities have not been confirmed. But we are in the process of corroborating several reports," she retorted firmly.

"Do you have any valid evidence implicating us in any crimes? Or do you just know that we were in cities of populations of several million each?"

The agent hesitated before finally saying, "No. Which is why you haven't been placed under arrest. But we would like to—"

"Then we're finished here, agent," Vince interrupted, rising from his seat and heading to the door. He ignored her protests as he knocked softly at first, before increasing the force, impatiently waiting for someone to let him out.

Someone did let him out, though he wasn't allowed to depart. A row of agents escorted him further through the complex to another office, Vince knowing better than to attempt to continue his protest as he succumbed to their pressure. They waited outside the door for some time before being joined by Noah, bearing an expression Vince could only have described as quizzical. The door was then finally opened and they were ushered inside.

The person to whom they were delivered came as a surprise and a relief. In a chair around a horseshoe table, legs crossed and expression stern, sat Secretary of State Maria Sanchez. She dressed in her usual arrangement of shades of blue, a pair of rimless rectangular glasses resting upon her nose.

"Vince," she greeted curtly. "And Noah Cox. We haven't met."

"It's a pleasure to meet you," Noah retained his politeness despite the irregularity of the situation, while Vince maintained an aura of caution.

"Is it?" Maria snapped. She ordered the lingering agents to leave the room before continuing. "Because three directors on the New Orion board have gone missing in the past few months. You two have been questioned. And I just got off the phone with Oliver Maddox.”

She narrowed her eyes and stepped closer, lowering her voice to an aggressive whisper.

“I am fully aware of Maddox’s plans. And I am not about to step in the way. In fact, it’s in my interest that they go ahead. What I don’t like is being out of the loop.”

“You know the way this job works, Maria,” Vince exclaimed. “I can’t just tell you when someone hires me for American targets. It’s not my decision to make. Sounds to me like your grievance is with Maddox.”

“What about you, Vince? Do you like being out of the loop?” She ignored him and carried on. “I wouldn’t guess so. So how would you like a little bit of information? Information about the European woman I saved you from?”

Vince’s eyes lit up and he nodded slowly. “What do you know about that?”

“The name of her employer, for one. The objective of said employer. Said employer’s home address, even. How would you like to know all that?”

“You make it sound like there’s a catch.”

“No catch. You just have to take him out. He’s the reason you’re here now, and I had to risk a damn lot to make sure you weren’t arrested. He was the one who gave you up, Vince. Anonymously, or so he thought. Gave your full name as a suspect behind the New Orion disappearances.”

Vince cursed. “How did he know?”

“I don’t know, but he tipped off the FBI not even two days ago. My guess is that this European woman who attacked you was his agent, and she managed to get your name, so it was easy enough for him to pass it on to the FBI. His name is Taylor Carrillo, senator for Nebraska. Lives in Omaha. You need to be more careful, Vince, because you're now prime suspect in an active investigation. You can't let them get even a whisker of evidence."

"We're professionals, Maria. A little bit of faith would be nice," Vince stated. "Thank you. How about we go visit Taylor Carrillo?"

CHAPTER 11

The agents that had interviewed Vince and Noah were visibly disgruntled as the pair exited the building alongside Maria. They retrieved their belongings from reception, re-inserting their neural chips and driving back to the McCarthy Tower where their own vehicles awaited. Vince proceeded to unlock his phone after the last of the FBI vehicles had departed and dialled a number he had obtained several years beforehand.

"Yeah?" an unenthusiastic voice grated after several rings.

"Hey, Leo. It's Vince. I need some work done."

"You want pick up or drop off?"

"I'm in Austin. Do you have a depot here?"

"Fuck, no. I know a guy in San Antonio who would do as good a job as me, though. Otherwise nearest I've got is Denver."

"Denver is fine."

"And what'll it be? I'm happy to pick it up from Austin, but it'll cost you."

"I'll drop it off. Thank you, Leo."

"Alright then."

The connection dropped abruptly and Vince filed into the F-150, Noah tailing him in a bronze Honda Accord as they began the long journey to Denver, Colorado. They stopped only once at a motel in Amarillo for a few hours of sleep before carrying on in the early hours of the morning.

The destination to which they arrived on the outskirts of Denver was a gated scrapyard full of cars, vans, and other myriad vehicles stacked dangerously high. The gate remained closed for a short while after their arrival as a man hobbled over from a hut hidden behind one of the stacks. One of his legs had been replaced by a cheap prosthetic, an older static model which didn't hook into the nervous system.

"Open!" the man could be heard calling as he approached. "Open! Stupid fucking gate, open!"

The gate finally complied with the man's raspy commands as it rattled slowly open and Vince pulled into the yard with Noah.

"How's it going, Vince? Is it this?" Leonardo Harrison, only ever addressed as Leo, reached up to shake Vince's hand in the elevated seat of the F-150.

"And behind. You've met Noah, haven't you?"

"I believe briefly. Good to see you again." Leo turned his attention to Noah as he then parked up at a much lower elevation than Vince. "Alright then, what's it gonna be this time?"

"Need them completely disappeared. Plate, tracker, the lot," Vince declared. "We're bordering on fugitives, as it happens."

"Oh, so you think to come in and incriminate my business? Nice one, Vince. Good going."

"We're not fugitives yet, you old sod, so you're fine. And the cars aren't registered to us. They belong to our employer, and he bought them with fake names."

"And he's happy for you to go scrapping his cars? I don't want to go stepping on any toes, Vince, especially not the types who hire you."

"He has plenty of cars to go round. How much do I owe you?"

Leo waved a hand. "I'll take them off you for free. They're basically new, for God's sake. Damn shame they have to go, but I'll make good money off the parts. I take it you'll want a replacement, though?"

"Something old, if you have it." Vince nodded in affirmation.

"Oh, I've got just the thing. Come with me."

Leo hobbled through the yard, turning what should have been a two-minute walk into five, but Vince wasn't bothered. The result at the end made it worth it.

"Feast your eyes. I've never had anything so nice anywhere near my lot," Leo said proudly, physically swelling with pride as he gestured to a car taking the centrepiece of an empty ring of ground.

What stood before them was in every way an antique, its age surpassing that of Vince's Mercedes by three decades.

"'93 Miata." Leo beamed as he placed a hand gingerly on the car's pristine black bonnet. "Seats are the original tan leather—real stuff, not like what they use nowadays. Only 116 horses, but this thing is light, real light. Twenty-two hundred pounds. Y'all Europeans would say a nice round metric tonne. I've replaced the lights, the exhaust, brake pads, et cetera—just about everything to keep it running and run it does. This car does not disappoint for something so old, and—get this—it only has a hundred thousand miles on it. I'm telling you, Vince, you want this. I hesitate to let it go."

"Not very low profile, is it?" Noah chimed in, him and Vince pacing curiously around the car.

Leo raised a finger and shook his head, grinning. "It might not be physically—or audibly—low profile, but it lacks something you find in every single modern car."

"An internet connection," Vince mused.

"Damn straight. Only waves coming to this car are radio, and that's only if you're lucky enough to be somewhere where a station still exists. There's a cassette player, if you really want some entertainment, but I don't suppose you've got many cassettes lying around, heh. Wouldn't be surprised if you didn't even know what a cassette was—they were dying out around about the time I was a youngin myself, and God, I rue the thought of how long ago that was."

"The steering wheel is on the right," Vince suddenly exclaimed, his eyes lighting up.

"Oh, yes, I was leaving that tidbit for last, though of course you can see it. This car is an import from your very own UR. Stick-shift, but you drive one of those back home, don't you?"

"I do, but nothing as beautiful as this." Vince's mouth hung open in awe. "I couldn't take it from you, Leo."

"Oh, it would not be cheap," Leo chuckled. "But it's not right to just sit here. And I'm a businessman, anyways. Buy and sell. That's what I do."

Vince turned to Leo and drew a deep breath. "Can I take it for a ride?"

The engine roared to life as he turned the key in the ignition and a smile creased his face as the roar diminished to a low, rumbling growl. He depressed the clutch and shifted into first, Noah clambering eagerly into the passenger seat with a face of pure envy.

"You can have a go afterwards," Vince said, releasing the clutch and pulling away.

They manoeuvred through the scrapyard as if it was a rally course, Vince having already made his decision about the purchase of the car. He wasn't worried about damaging it—he was confident in his ability.

The tyres squealed as he burst out onto the main road through the desolate desert landscape and the whole car hummed with the speed to which he rapidly accelerated. Seventy, eighty, ninety miles per hour, the sparse scenery turning to a blur, the wind rippling through his hair and roaring past his ears. They remained alert to the possibility of a stray police car but weren't really afraid. Nothing could hide in the flat, barren fields east of Denver.

They returned to the scrapyard an hour later more out of necessity than desire, the fuel needle dangling dangerously close to empty.

"Name your price, Leo," Vince insisted, stepping out of the car and gently closing the door.

"Two-fifty," the old man said, his tone indicating no place for haggling. "And you promise me that you don't destroy her."

"You have my word." They shook hands and Vince paid in cryptocurrency via his neural chip.

As they were pulling out of the scrapyard, he brought the car to a sudden halt before stepping out and rushing back over to Leo.

"One more thing," he said, grabbing the old man's shoulder. "The tracker on the F-150. Do you think I could take it with me?"

He and Noah had arrived in Omaha before the day's end.

CHAPTER 12

"Oliver."

"Maria. How did it go?"

"Agents asked them a few questions, they refused to answer anything and stormed out. They were brought to me after that. I told them about Carrillo and they went on their way."

"Good. I've got tabs on their cars and they're headed to Denver. No idea why, but I assume they'll carry on to Omaha from there. You're sure they'll kill him?"

"Without a doubt. If there's one thing you need to know about Vince, it's that he doesn't do half measures."

"All it takes is a few words from Carrillo to turn us over. Then what's stopping him from letting him go and coming after us, instead?"

"What part of 'no half measures' did you not understand? Carrillo isn't even going to see him. You know how he dealt with the directors that have gone missing already. None of our intelligence agencies have been able to corroborate a case against him. Lots of CCTV footage of him in the areas where they disappeared but no DNA, no direct evidence of the crimes, nothing to implicate him or Noah or you in anything."

"And what about that Arab Vince roped in to help him? What happened to him?"

"Carrillo's guy got him. I didn't tell Vince that but I'm sure he knows, and I'm surprised he didn't ask me about it. She must have got Vince's name out him—you didn't give him anyone else, right?"

Oliver Maddox took a long drag on a cigar before coughing and answering. "No. Just the Arab. He wasn't meant to know there was more than one."

"Well, Carrillo's guy went after Vince and was amateur enough to let him keep his neural chip in. Police caught her and she escaped back to Europe after Carrillo paid her bail. I don't get this plan of yours, Oliver. Why not just include Vince so you don't risk pissing him off?"

"Because I'm sending someone to kill him at the end of it all. Do you know how much he's charging? That man is extorting me! I keep him in the dark and it'll be a lot easier when the time comes to get rid of him."

"Whatever you do, make damned sure that I'm not implicated. I don't want to suffer because of any mistakes you make."

"Mistakes I make..." Maddox snickered. "Don't worry, Maria, it'll all be very clean. Maybe not Vince Foster levels of clean, but it'll be about a hundred times cheaper. And you have the influence to clean up any mess. Don't bullshit me."

"I think you overestimate just how far my power stretches. I'm Secretary of State, not the god-damned President. Hell, even the President doesn't have that sort of reach. I know democracy might be dead in London, but here in the U.S. it is still alive and well. Rife with corruption, maybe, but alive."

"Yeah, alright," Maddox said dismissively. "I'll update you when they get to Omaha."

Maria was left facing her reflection before she even had a chance to offer her own farewell.

CHAPTER 13

Instead of staying at one of Oliver Maddox's many residences, Vince opted for an unimpressive, aging three-star hotel squeezed amongst a swathe of modern high-rises. It didn't offer any parking and he had to drive to an adjacent block to find a garage where he felt confident the vehicle wouldn't be stolen.

Taylor Carrillo was a family man. That was the opening line in the document he had been sent by Maria. Fierce defender of the Second Amendment and rabid conspiracy theorist, too. Also a very successful businessman, meaning that he could afford to renovate his home in the upmarket neighbourhood of Regency with enough security devices to ensure he was the last man standing in the case of the apocalypse.

Cameras, motion sensors, high fences, biometric locks. Vince concluded before he and Noah had even begun that they would not be confronting him at his home.

Difficulties arose from the fact that his home was also his place of work. Taylor Carrillo was rare in not living in or near D.C., instead choosing to connect remotely to Senate sessions.

"We can't loiter around here," Noah said as the pair of them sat in the car, parked in the shade of the oak trees planted methodically around the ring forming the end of Carrillo's cul-de-sac. "Especially not in this. I've already seen people staring out their windows at us. Look, it's happening right now."

Noah nodded in the direction of the house adjacent to Taylor Carrillo's and Vince followed his gaze to spot an old man peering through the break in the pair of blinds shrouding vision through a colossal ground-floor window.

"Nothing about this can be done the traditional way." Vince turned the key in the ignition and the expression barely visible on the old man's face turned from scrutiny to contempt, the silent street lit up with sound as they pulled away.

"I looked into this guy," Noah said. "He's a big shareholder in New Orion. Company was private under the last owner, but he died ten years ago and ownership went to his son. The son went public with the company to raise money to get to the moon and our Taylor Carrillo bought a thirty-percent stake. And the directors we're dealing with—"

"Were appointed by him," Vince inferred, which Noah confirmed with a nod. "Who else has a stake?"

"Nobody really relevant. Carrillo gets plenty of flak politically for conflict of interest, because he's always advocating that new NASA contracts go to New Orion. Which is fair enough, their competitors don't really hold a candle to them. But he always manages to brush it off. He's a dirty player, which might well explain the paranoia. I found his voting record, too. He's a veritable Luddite. Voted against the approval of android workers, against 8G, against self-driving vehicles, neural chips, it goes on and on. Where are we going?"

Vince slowed down and spun the wheel to perform a harsh U-turn. "Back to Carrillo's. I have an idea."

He parked a couple blocks over from the cul-de-sac and they walked the remaining distance, putting on masks and sunglasses as they turned into the street.

"Hello, Vince?" Noah urged. "Have you forgotten about the cameras?"

"There won't be any inside. And if he voted against neural chips, and rails against the premise in general, then I don't reckon he'll have one himself."

They stepped onto the stones leading up to the whitewashed wood patio, gazing around at the series of cameras bearing down upon them from atop the high mesh fence. One final camera built into the doorbell awaited them at the front door, where Vince casually knocked and stepped back, waiting.

The response was almost immediate. The voice over the speakers, situated in all four corners the veranda's roof, was measured, nonchalant—not how Vince had imagined someone with a reputation for paranoia. "Identify yourselves. Name and reason for visit."

"Felix Weißmann," Vince answered in a practised German accent. "And this is my associate Matteo Schulz. Are we speaking to Mr Carrillo?"

"Reason for visit." Each word was enunciated with an obstinate gap in between.

"We've come to speak with Mr Carrillo. We're entrepreneurs from Hamburg who have just founded a moon mining software development firm. We thought he may be interested in an investment and lobbying opportunity—we're in dire need of support in your American Senate."

A brief silence ensued in which Vince found himself losing hope in the workability of his slapdash plan. That hope was then in an instant restored with the swinging open of the front door, before being again unrelentingly torn away.

The man who stood before them cocked an assault shotgun and pointed it between the pair of them at such a position that the shrapnel would have shred them both with a single shot. Wielding the weapon was a Hispanic man matching the images Vince and Noah had already seen in preparation.

"So you think that you can just rock on up to my home address peddling some 'investment opportunity'?" The mediation with which he had spoken over the intercom had vanished. "I don't believe you for a second. What's your real names? Tell me right this god-damned second before I exercise my right to defend my property."

"We are telling the truth, Mr Carrillo." Vince was un-flinching in the rapidity of his response and the confidence with which he delivered it. "We did not think you would be in your official office so we took the initiative to come to see you in person. To show you that we really mean business. I have always found that a face-to-face conver-sation achieves much more than a video link. Please, for-give me for the intrusion."

Carrillo stepped closer and shifted his aim from the pair of them exclusively onto Vince, butting the end of the shotgun into his chest. "I don't know how things work in Europe, wherever the hells you two are from, but you don't walk onto a man's property unannounced and expect a warm embrace when you're in the States. You get out of here right now and I might not shoot y'all in the back as soon as you turn tail."

Vince glanced at Noah, who understood at once the look in his eyes. The gun still trained on Vince, Noah whipped his pistol out of its concealed holster and placed the end of its silencer against Taylor Carrillo's temple. The senator was quickly absolved of confidence, his face turn-ing to a terrified grimace as he quickly came to realise the sudden tipping of the scales.

"Put that down," Noah spoke. "Slowly."

Carrillo was unmoving as he stared at Vince, eyes alight with pure venom. "Felix my ass. I know you. You're Vince Foster. The guy hunting the New Orion directors."

The hitman's eyes fell through his sunglasses to the camera on the doorbell and he refrained from response.

"I ought to rip a hole through you right now," the senator continued to seethe, Noah nudging his head with the pistol to remind him of its presence.

"Put the gun down," he repeated.

Carrillo finally complied, the barrel of the shotgun falling from Vince's chest as the senator crouched, with a laboured grunt, to lay it upon the wooden panels of the patio. Vince picked up the weapon and slung it over his shoulder as he and Noah corralled the senator into the house.

"Are there any more cameras?" He looked with apprehension around the house as they found their way into a living room, where he issued a command to turn on the television. "Microphones? Anything?"

"I'm not saying a word to you," Carrillo retorted. Though defiant, his expression and demeanour betrayed anxiety, though evidently not derived from his capture.

A sudden noise resonated from upstairs. Footsteps. Vince and Noah concealed themselves behind the walls as the footsteps transitioned to the stairwell and thundered down without restraint. They then just as abruptly stopped, as a prepubescent voice uttered, "Dad?"

A boy. The hitmen knew that Carrillo had children—two boys and a girl. They had been counting on the fact that they would have been at school.

Carrillo, sitting on the sofa with a direct view out into the hallway where the stairwell was situated, looked bleak as he responded. "Hey, buddy. Dad's busy right now—why don't you go head on back upstairs and I'll come see you in a minute?"

"Who were you talking to?" the boy inquired.

Vince looked at Noah and they communicated wordlessly.

Noah removed his mask and sunglasses and then emerged from his cover, silently holstering his gun. "Hello, little man. We're just working out some business with your dad, my partner and I. Mr Carrillo, you didn't tell us your son would be home."

"He's sick," the senator mumbled.

"Oh, you poor thing." Noah looked with tangible concern to the boy that Vince still couldn't see as he removed the shotgun from his shoulder, leaning it against the adjacent wall, and then removing his own disguise. "Mr Carrillo—why don't I go look after him while you conclude your business with my associate?"

Vince then joined Noah in the entryway, finally laying his eyes upon the unexpected arrival and smiling.

"I don't know—"

"Come on, then. What's your name?"

Noah sauntered towards the stairs and ushered the boy away, flashing his gun as they disappeared. Vince turned around and unholstered his own pistol, holding it idly on his lap as he took a seat across from Carrillo.

"Are there any more recording devices?"

"No. Not inside the house." The senator looked at the floor as he spoke.

He dropped the German accent. "And your wife? Is she going to make any sudden appearances?"

"She's gone on a business trip. Not gonna be back today."

"Good." Vince stood up and paced across the room. "How did you find out that we were hunting New Orion directors?"

"It—it was just standard procedure. Corporate security," Carrillo stammered. "I was protecting my interests. Whoever hired you, I don't believe they're the only person who wants to load the board with their own cronies or otherwise make a mess of operations."

"Corporate security in the form of a privately hired European hitwoman? One willing to practise torture to get information for you? That's not corporate security. You knew about Hamzah. Only question is how. There are several questions beginning with how, actually. How did you know about Hamzah? How did you know where to send your agent? How did you know that he was targeting New Orion directors?"

Carrillo licked his lips and steadied his breathing, tapping his foot irritably against the hardwood floor. "I can't tell you. He'd kill me if he found out."

"I'll kill you if you don't speak," Vince said placidly.

The only sound for some time was the muted clattering of footsteps and the droning of news on the television as Carrillo mulled his options.

"You have to protect me," he said. "I rat him out and you have to make sure he doesn't send someone just like you to kill me without this negotiation business beforehand."

"You're not the one calling the shots." Vince exemplified his authority with a cursory glance to the ceiling.

"You're a heartless son of a bitch. I hope you know that."

"Who tipped you off?"

Carrillo hesitated again, before finally saying, "One of the London oligarchs. Oliver Maddox."

Vince stopped pacing and stood momentarily still as an indescribable pang of emotion wrenched his gut. He had felt such a sensation only in times of deep regret—this was different. He had never felt such raw betrayal and the uninvited fury that accompanied it.

"It seems we've both been betrayed, Mr Carrillo," Vince said measuredly. "Oliver Maddox is the man who hired me."

Carrillo finally peeled his eyes from the floor and looked at Vince with shared realisation and an unspoken mending of the tension that had been enacted.

Noah, come down here, Vince dictated in a message via his neural chip, and the pair were reunited with his appearance.

"Are we finished?"

"No," Vince said coldly. "We've only just begun."

Noah didn't conceal his confusion. "Care to explain?"

"Your boss tipped you off," Carrillo cut in, the hollowness that had dominated his voice until that point absent. "To me. I thought he was helping me out, letting me know that somebody was hunting my directors. But he's pulling strings all around, so it's turned out. Stabbed you right in the back."

"Hamzah died because Maddox led his agent straight to him," Vince elaborated. "And then to me. Right from the beginning, he's been working against us. Playing both sides. Devious little bastard."

"He'll find out, you know?" Carrillo's voice trembled even more so than when Noah had gone upstairs with his son. "He'll find out and then it'll be scorched earth for us. The moment you step out of that door and I'm still alive, he sends his goons to track us down and kill us. Much like he sent you to kill me, Vince. Except this time, they wouldn't be looking for vengeance. It'd be a cold-blooded contract killing, pure and simple."

Vince resumed his pacing, rubbing his head in contemplation. "You're right—he can't know that I let you live. So what if you died?"

The senator squinted at him incomprehensibly. "Come again?"

"We fake your death," he elaborated, his hand falling from his head into exaggerated gestures. "For all intents and purposes, you are dead. You go missing, just as I would approach any contract. That's what Maddox'll be expecting. That places us several steps ahead of him, because as far as he knows, this plan of his—whatever the hell it is—is falling into place. Which provides us with a valuable opportunity to get to him in person, away from the private army, before he has any suspicion of our knowledge."

"You're missing one crucial point," Noah chimed in. "If he betrayed us, there's no way he was ever expecting to stay on our good sides. He never intended to pay us that bounty money. We're dead to him. We step foot in his office or near his house and we'll be executed."

"He's not hunting us yet," Vince argued. "We have no evidence to suggest that that phase of his plan has begun. So we act quickly, before it can even happen."

"And what are we meant to say when we rock up to the CSC headquarters and ask for a meeting? He'll have been tracking us all this time. What's stopping him from tracking us a little bit more?"

"The fact that the F-150's tracker will be attached to the underside of whatever car I find at the nearest high-end hotel. He'll be tracking 'us' while we hone in on him in London. We'll catch him by surprise."

"You're confident, Vince," Noah exclaimed. "As always."

"If I may interject," Carrillo spoke up after a while. "We appear to have glossed over the fact that you want me to 'die'. What exactly did you have in mind for this?"

"We'll fake your death," Vince reiterated assuredly. "That won't be difficult. We just need to keep you somewhere safe while we make our move. While the media reports on your disappearance, Maddox quietly chuckling to himself, we'll be enacting our revenge."

"And how long do you think that'll take? I have a family, Vince. I need to be there for them."

"Your choice is to wait around and spend a few weeks away from them or never be there for them again. Which do you prefer?"

CHAPTER 14

The trio exited Carrillo's house, all donning disguises before loading into the front of Carrillo's cherry-red Dodge Ram, which roared to life with the artificial sound of an internal combustion engine. Vince drove, while Carrillo crouched beneath the glovebox, concealing his face. Their destination was the hotel where he and Noah had stayed under their fake German names.

They pulled up in front of the hotel and Vince was the first to hop down onto the tarmac, gesturing for the other two to stay put. He swept his eyes over the surrounding street, spotting several cameras watching the entrances to nearby premises and swiftly disabling them with his infrared laser. He then proceeded into the hotel lobby itself, approaching the teenager working the front desk, his face stricken with boredom that didn't abate with Vince's arrival.

"Yeah?" he droned uninterestedly, scrolling robotically through his phone.

"Where do you guys store the CCTV footage from the cameras? Is it on a machine in this building or on the cloud?"

The receptionist shrugged. "Could be. Not my place to say. Who are you, anyways?"

Vince exhaled sharply in exasperation. "Do you have a manager I can talk to, then?"

"Owner is somewhere in the back, probably."

"Well, can you go get them?"

The receptionist wrenched himself out of his chair and groaned, making a sound reminiscent of someone thirty years his senior, before sauntering through a door behind the desk and allowing it to slam shut behind him. Vince leaned forwards, craning his neck to look at the various screens littering the cluttered desk, one of them hosting the remarkably low-resolution feeds from the security cameras dotted around the building's interior. He leaned further to get a view of the desk's underside, where he could see only a half-full waste bin and the PC connected to the monitors on the desk.

He flinched back to stand unassumingly in front of the desk as the door swung open, crashing unyieldingly into a stopper nailed loosely into the adjacent wall. The receptionist returned to his seat, trailed by a permanently grumpy man bearing remarkable physical resemblance to

Bobby Vegas. Except for his accent which, though comparably thick, was Louisianan.

"Kai here says you're asking about where we keep the camera footage?" He trained his eyes inquisitively, scrutinisingly, upon Vince. "What do y'all need to know about that for?"

"I work for a cloud company," Vince lied. "I was hoping to discuss your storage arrangements with you. Assuming you still use physical storage for the video data, your company could save a lot of money storing it remotely. Some of the rates you can get in the new communist states are really attractive—they're desperate for the investment."

"Well, I'm sorry to burst your bubble, whoever you are, but we're not interested. Things work perfectly well the way they are."

"Please, I must insist—at least let me have a conversation with you about it. I know I'm a salesman and you probably have your notions about what salesmen are like but what I'm proposing is a genuinely mutually beneficial arrangement. And we offer a free trial. When I say you'll save money from this arrangement, I really mean it."

The hotel's owner drew a long breath and shook his head, blinking. "Oh, I guess I can spare a few minutes. Don't mess me around."

He gestured Vince around the desk and through the door from which he had emerged, leading him to a decrepit office with stained yellow walls and raggedy carpet, offering him a seat in a worn faux leather armchair. He tentatively took his place in the seat, the hotel's owner sitting across from him in a mesh swivel chair which looked luxurious amid its rundown surroundings.

"I'm River. River Quinn," Vince said, proffering his hand.

"Lazlo," the hotel manager replied, wheezing as he stretched to meet Vince's gesture. "Let's hear it then. I'm not such a techie guy so explain it to me in terms I'll understand—money."

Vince nodded and smiled. "Basically, my firm offers cloud storage solutions. We mediate between you, the client, and our providers—we have centres bidding in Southeast Asia, most stable African countries, and lots of South America. Running a server here in the U.S. isn't cheap, as I'm sure you know—how much is your electricity bill, if you don't mind me asking?"

"I do mind a little bit... how about y'all name some sort of price range for this cloud storage? And how much do I have to do as far as management goes?"

"Would it be possible to get a look at the server? That way I can give you a much better estimate of what we're looking at."

Lazlo didn't get up, nodding his head towards the corner of the room. "I let the kid deal with stuff like that. He knows more than me. But that's the machine."

Vince had spotted the server when they had entered the room but stood up and moved to inspect it now that he had express confirmation.

"Is this used for all the hotel's systems and data?"

"Pretty sure. We don't have any others. Some stuff I just keep on my tablet. The kid stores some on his chip for convenience."

The hitman slid his fingers behind the back of the server rack, pretending to inspect it. "Are the cameras hardwired to the network?"

"I dunno. Maybe?" Lazlo then raised his voice to say, "Kai! Get in here!"

The receptionist appeared perhaps thirty seconds later, eyes still glued to his phone screen. "Yeah?"

"Guy has a question for you. What was it?"

"The cameras," Vince repeated. "Are they hardwired to the server? There's only one ethernet cable connected here."

"Yeah, that's it. Everything else is on the Wi-Fi," Kai confirmed.

"How do you get the footage on the front desk?"

"Server streams the feed to the computer out front."

"Alright. That helps, thanks."

Kai nodded and departed, Vince cursing in his head and rethinking his strategy.

"So? How much money could I save?" Lazlo asked disinterestedly.

"A server like this with the amount of data you're using could probably be set up for about... I would estimate fifty dollars per month, all in," he supplied, plucking a number out of thin air. "And we'll buy the server off you, if you so desire. I could even get started right now. What do you say?"

Lazlo stood up and reached to shake Vince's hand. "Well, I'd be crazy to pass that up. Mr Quinn, you've got yourself a deal. Where do I sign?"

"Oh, don't worry about that just now. I'll arrange some paperwork and send it over after I'm done the preliminary work here. Do you mind if I fiddle around with your wires for a bit?"

"Not at all. Can I get you a coffee or something?"

"Yes, actually. Americano, if you don't mind."

Lazlo waddled to the coffee machine and amalgamation of mugs in various states, all situated on an old plywood table positioned precariously close to the server rack. In the meantime, Vince wandered back out into the lobby, crawling under the desk to examine the back of the PC hosting the displays above him.

"I'm going to have to disconnect the security feed for a moment," he said, directing his gaze at Kai. The receptionist nodded laxly and Vince proceeded back into the server room, where Lazlo shoved a cup of cheap ersatz coffee into his hands. He reached back and disconnected the ethernet cable connecting the CCTV cameras to the network and quickly checked out front to ensure that the feed had ceased to appear on the monitor on the front desk, which it had.

Noah, he dictated through his neural chip. *The cameras are down. I need you to bring him in now. Third floor, room 31.*

Noah and Carrillo passed swiftly through the hotel's front doors and reached the stairwell before Kai had even looked up to take notice of the chiming of the bell.

Vince returned again to the office and took a sip from the coffee, masking his disgust with neutrality as Lazlo took his seat, the chair whining, and browsed aimlessly through a tablet he revealed from one of the drawers in his desk.

A message came from Noah just as Vince was about to plug the security feed back in, reading, *We need your keycard.*

The hitman set his coffee down and withdrew from the office, uttering a curt, "Excuse me for one moment," before proceeding up the stairs and handing over the key card to unlock the room.

"Nobody's seen either of you?" he asked.

"No," Noah confirmed. "What's the plan now?"

Vince entered the room with the pair of them and the door slid closed.

"I'm going to wrap things up downstairs and then drive your car somewhere it won't be found for a while," he directed his attention to Carrillo, who nodded sombrely. "Does anyone have access to the tracker information?"

"Tracker? I removed that damned thing the moment it left the dealership."

"Excellent. Well, Mr Carrillo, you are now, for all intents and purposes, dead. That is the narrative we want to portray. You cannot contact anyone. You cannot leave this room. You can use your phone, as long as you use a VPN. If you don't follow these rules, you put yourself at risk of being found by Maddox and that puts us at risk, too."

"Can't I just send one message to my wife?" he pleaded. "Let her know everything'll be okay? That I haven't packed up and left her?"

"No," Vince said curtly. "Dead men don't send messages to their wives. Once Maddox is dead, you can come out of hiding. But until then, you stay here, a ghost. Noah will provide you with food and water and everything else you need. And his name, to you, is no longer Noah. It is Matteo, Matteo Schulz. Once you're reported as missing, your truck included, the first thing police will do is check plate recognition data, and realise that I've taken it out of town. They will catch on to the fact that it's been parked outside this hotel today and they'll send someone to inspect. Matteo will deal with it, and you will comply fully with whatever he needs you to do. Is that understood?"

"Just kill the bastard, Vince. I don't wanna stay cooped up here any longer than I have to."

"I will try my best. It's a formidable task. Anyone have any questions before I wrap things up downstairs and turn the cameras back on?"

"I do," Noah said. "One thing, Vince. Would you mind checking in on Ruth? I've been away a while and I want her to see a friendly face in person."

Vince was about to say no but then hesitated and nodded. "Fine, briefly. After I've dealt with Maddox."

They said their final goodbyes and Vince returned to the lobby, entering the office and replacing the ethernet cable supplying the camera feed.

"So the setup is a little more complicated than I anticipated," he lied to Lazlo, downing the rest of the ersatz coffee with a grimace. "I'll have to come back another time with the right tools. But the first month will be free, and we can arrange payment after that. How's that sound?"

The hotel owner cracked a smile and shook Vince's hand one last time. "That's perfect. You just give us a call to sort out when's a good time for you. It's been a pleasure."

"Likewise," the hitman said. "I'll see you soon."

Lazlo never saw Vince again.

CHAPTER 15

Vince spent the rest of the day driving along the Missouri River, leaving Carrillo's pickup parked at the side of the road halfway between Omaha and the nearby town of Fort Calhoun. He then called a taxi to take him back to Omaha before booking a private flight to London under the name Felix Weißmann, departing the same day from the O'Hare International Airport in Chicago. He couldn't bear to abandon the Mazda, though, and paid for long-term parking in a block in the city under his real name.

He booked into a hotel immediately after touchdown and programmed himself to sleep until the morning of the following day to reset his circadian rhythm.

Vince was never going to be able to reach Maddox in his own headquarters. He knew it before boarding the plane to London and he knew it as he left the hotel and beckoned for a taxi to take him to an office on the bank of the Thames in Canary Wharf.

Nobody could rule without allies. And the oligarchy manipulating the strings of independent London was no different. Maddox, while the most powerful and influential member of the city's deep state, relied on other oligarchs, puppet politicians, and covert informants to maintain his uncontested position at the head of the Camden Space Corporation. This was no secret, and neither was the fact that he had enemies who wanted to bring him down.

One such enemy was Montgomery Sharp, director of competing space travel firm Sharpspace and major shareholder in the privatised National Health Service. Their rivalry was notorious, with Maddox and his larger share in the health service resulting in policy clashes that had long since boiled into a lasting feud between the pair.

The taxi ride lasted an hour and Vince would have, under normal circumstances, opted for a helitaxi. The problem with that was Maddox's part ownership of the company with a monopoly over London's network of premium helitaxis.

A crowd of tourists and businesspeople in equal measure thronged the riverside as usual. Engineers, accountants, contractors, and financiers flowed constantly into and out of the imposing glass-walled Sharpspace offices. Vince was one face amongst many, and yet he felt deeply unsettled as he gazed with his disguised face into the camera nestled above the reception desk to watch over the entryway.

"Welcome to Sharpspace. How can I help?" the android sitting behind the desk asked as Vince approached.

"I'd like to arrange a meeting with Mr Sharp," the hitman said cautiously, warily unconfident of his ability to socially engineer an android.

"Could I get your name, please?"

"Felix Weißmann."

"And who are you representing?"

"Myself. This is not a business meeting. This is something deeply personal. Please let the director know that this is about Oliver Maddox."

"I'm sorry, I'm afraid I don't understand," the android droned. "Mr Sharp's schedule is entirely full and it is impossible to arrange a meeting with him via this desk. Please reach out to someone in higher management and they will hopefully be able to help you at a later date."

Vince cursed and didn't continue his efforts, opening his phone and scrolling through his contacts until he came upon Maria, where he pressed to call her and waited.

"Vince?" her voice rasped after several rings.

"I need a phone number, Maria. I'm hoping you've got it," he said quickly, pacing around a free area in the Sharpspace lobby. "Montgomery Sharp. Do you have it?"

"Slow down, Vince. What do you need with Monty?"

"That doesn't matter. Do you have the number?"

"A chip number, he doesn't have a phone. What are you doing? Are you in London?"

"The number, Maria. Please send it to me."

Vince brought the phone down from his ear and hung up, a contact appearing shortly thereafter through his neural chip. He rang it without delay and was connected several seconds later.

"Who is this?" a voice as raspy as Maria's, though much deeper, grated.

"Mr Sharp, my name is Vince Foster. I'm currently stood in the reception of Sharpspace headquarters in London and I would really like to meet with you."

"I've never heard of you. What makes you worth my time?"

"I'm Oliver Maddox's hitman. He hired me to eliminate the New Orion leadership and then stabbed me in the back. I'm going to kill him, but I need help."

There was a pause, and then Montgomery spoke softly, "Tenth floor. I'll be waiting."

CHAPTER 16

Maria was on the phone to Maddox seconds after sending Montgomery Sharp's contact to Vince.

"Come on, come on, come on, you bastard," she muttered impatiently, standing up and pacing around her office.

"Maria. What is it now?" the oligarch sighed.

"Where is Vince, Oliver?" she asked sharply.

"Last I checked, driving around Omaha. Have you seen the news?"

"Yes, I've seen the news, I've spoken to the damned President about it. That's not what's important. How are you tracking Vince's location?"

"His car. I've got its GPS right here in front of my eyes."

"And what about Noah?"

"They left it in Denver. Stopped at a scrapyard, so I assume it's been turned to spare parts and they carried on together."

"Well, I just got a call from Vince. Do you want to take a stab at what it was about?"

"Don't fuck me around, Maria."

"Montgomery Sharp. How do you feel about him?"

Maddox snorted. "Insufferable bastard. What's this got to do with anything?"

"Vince asked for his number. No details, sounded like he was in a real hurry. Wouldn't answer any of my questions. Have you caught him on any of your cameras? Informants?"

"And you gave it to him?"

"Of course I did!" she exclaimed. "What did you want me to do?"

"Say no? Whatever, this situation is manageable. I've got guys in Sharpspace. They see him, they'll tell me right away. I'll send someone to check out that tracker in the meantime."

Maria tried to respond, but Maddox had already hung up.

CHAPTER 17

"Mr Foster. A pleasure to meet you."

Montgomery Sharp, or Monty, as he insisted to be called, was as imposing as the offices over which he reigned. Standing over two metres tall with an impressively full head of hair for a man of seventy years, Vince was embarrassed to have to look up to meet his eyes as they shook hands. His voice was deep and silky and he moved with a strangely hypnotic fluidity—Vince realised later that it was, in fact, unnatural, the oligarch having equipped himself with several cybernetic implants to aid movement.

"Likewise," Vince said. "I have a proposal for you, Monty, and time is of the essence, so I'd appreciate it if we hurried things along. How do you feel about Oliver Maddox?"

"I think you know how I feel about Oliver Maddox. I make no secret of it," Monty replied. "I think the more important question is how you feel about Oliver Maddox. And why it's led you to my office. So please, elaborate. How exactly did he betray you?"

"He was pulling strings behind my back to get me to do an important job without ever intending to pay me. And then he was working with someone to undermine me while at the same time trying to get me to kill him. He pitted us against each other. As things stand, I'm a step ahead. But I'm not naïve enough to think that will remain the case. You've seen the news about the disappearance of Taylor Carrillo?"

Monty sipped a cup of herbal tea and nodded before replying, "The American senator? I heard something of the sort."

"A friend of mine is keeping watch of him in a hotel in Omaha. The police aren't going to find him, but Maddox very well might. And I don't even trust Carrillo not to give the game up himself. I need to kill Maddox before he realises that I'm onto him. I was hoping you could help with that."

Monty raised his eyebrows and then delicately set down his tea. "You're very bold to meet me and come immediately forward with such a proposal. It is no small feat."

"I'm quite aware, but I don't have a lot of time," Vince emphasised. "Was I wrong to assume you would be interested in my proposal?"

"Let's not be so hasty. I hardly know you, Vince Foster. What's to convince me that you're not just an agent working for Oliver Maddox? He has plenty of those."

"I am an agent working for Oliver Maddox. That's why I'm your best opportunity to take out your biggest rival—don't pretend that you don't want to be rid of him."

"Oh, I want to be rid of him. But I don't immediately trust anyone who walks into my office. You're a hitman—I'm sure you can understand that nobody should award trust so easily. And in my world, where all anyone is ever trying to do is undermine their fellow man, you can surely understand that such distrust is standard."

"I understand fully. I operate entirely within your world. In all my life I have trusted exactly one person and I don't intend to trust any more. I never came to you expecting your immediate trust—all I request is your collaboration in the achievement of a mutually beneficial goal."

"Well," Monty said. "You lost your advantage over Maddox the moment you walked through the front doors. This building is riddled with his corporate spies, just as the CSC office is full of mine. He knows you're here and will prepare for any action from either of us. He's very well protected. Not often seen unguarded in public."

"Nobody is invulnerable. You're both major shareholders in the NHS—you must see him often enough?"

"Maddox usually votes by proxy or digitally. That's the case for most shareholders, though that's rather out of time efficiency than paranoia. In-person board meetings are exceedingly rare," Monty stated. "However, it's impossible for him to attend a gathering by proxy. If my calendar isn't lying, Christie West is hosting a soirée at her estate this coming Friday evening for Independence Day. Attending is one Oliver Maddox. He will of course be protected, even at the event. At no point will he let his guard down. But if we are going to strike, this is the time to do it. We must just outsmart him. I do not say that as if it is an easy task. I've spent the post-war period trying to do so. At no point have I ever succeeded."

"How many people will be there?" Vince inquired.

"Several hundred. If I've learned anything about Christie West in the few times that I've met her, it's that she does not shy away from extravagance."

"Sneak me in. As a guest, a member of the staff. Or I can sneak in myself. Where is her estate? How well protected is it?"

"Blenheim Palace in Oxfordshire. Christie erected a high fence around most of it after purchasing it from the government of the UR, but on its western side lies the River Glyme. You could cross this way, but I doubt you would do so unnoticed. I also doubt, though, that there will be excessive security. It is a party, after all."

"I need more details, Monty. I'll travel to the Palace today and scope it out—as for you, I need information. You have my chip number—any details at all pertaining to the party, the guests, the arrangements, times, absolutely anything that might be of use. I need it all."

"One moment, Vince," Monty cautioned. "How exactly do you intend to kill Maddox? And what will you do afterwards?"

"What do you think?" Vince raised an eyebrow. "A bullet to the head. I'm not doing this for the perverse pleasure some get from torture. I'm not doing it for information. It's pure and simple revenge. I'll kill him quickly and cleanly and then I'm going to fall off the face of the Earth."

"Very good. You are a professional." Monty gazed thoughtfully out of the window. "But sometimes professionals make mistakes. You understand I can have no ties to you in the event of a mishap, yes? Do you have a fabrication I can relay to the press and other interested parties?"

"I'm a freelance security consultant. That's my official job title, that's how I'm hired by anyone for any job. That's how the Treasury knows me. And that is, officially, how you know me. Now, I'll be on my way to Blenheim Palace. It's been a pleasure to meet you, Monty."

"Good luck, Mr Foster," Monty said, standing up and shaking Vince's hand. "Don't make a mess."

CHAPTER 18

"Here for Mr Maddox."

"Name, please," the woman at the reception desk asked drily, her eyes glued idly to her computer screen.

"Aurel Kostra."

The receptionist raised an eyebrow and glanced askance at the short-haired, stern-eyed man standing patiently before her. "How do you spell that, sorry?"

"A-U-R-E-L," the man spoke slowly, his Slovak accent unintelligibly thick. "K-O—"

"Oh, yes, I've got you here," the woman interrupted. "Head on up to floor seventy. He's waiting for you."

Oliver Maddox paced back and forth behind his desk with a cigar and a glass of whisky in his hands as Aurel emerged from the lift. He moved forward wordlessly to

131

greet the oligarch, who was the first to proffer a hand, which the Slovak shook firmly but briefly.

"You must be... Aurel? Am I pronouncing that right?"

"Aurel Kostra," Aurel enunciated.

"Yeah, no way am I ever getting the hang of that. I'll call you AK. Please, take a seat."

Aurel lowered himself into one of the minimalistic office chairs opposite the oligarch's monumental half-circle desk and Maddox downed the remainder of his whisky with a quick flourish.

"Let's not waste any time," he growled. "You know why you're here."

"A hit," Aurel replied nonchalantly.

"A very specific hit. A hit on another hitman. But you have to find him first."

"This is no problem."

"Good. Here's a profile."

Maddox slid an unlocked tablet across the table and Aurel gingerly picked it up, swiping through information appertaining to an individual by the name of Vince Foster. Aurel knew of him—his name was frequently thrown around in the criminal spheres in which the Slovak found most of his contracts. He had a reputation for ruthless efficiency and remarkable effectiveness. He had been in the game for far longer than Aurel. But Aurel was not deterred.

"Do you have any leads I can follow?"

"Several. The tracker on his partner's car died yesterday at a scrapyard in a city across the pond. The tracker on his car is apparently driving around Omaha, Nebraska, even though he's been spotted in London. He's in cahoots with

Montgomery Sharp, something of a rival of mine. And we put a tracker on his personal car, which, last time I checked, was still driving around London. There's a lot for you to investigate, but the first place you ought to be visiting is that scrapyard. Someone there spoke to Vince Foster and Noah Cox and we need to know why."

"Okay." Aurel nodded. "How much are you paying?"

"There's that question." Maddox raised a finger and shook it, smirking. "If you kill Vince, I'll give you a million dollars. But there is opportunity for more. If you can find Noah Cox and kill him first—it has to be first—then the reward is double. Two million for the both of them. Do we have a deal?"

"It is a deal," Aurel agreed, and the men shook hands once more. He then rose from his seat and, after exchanging contact details, departed.

Maddox had been generous enough to allow use of one of his private jets, which was the first time Aurel had ever travelled as such. His usual clients were often European politicians and businesspeople keenly aware of the close watch under which they were kept by the all-encompassing Federal Security Service empowered in the wake of the war. To operate in London and America was a luxury he had not yet been afforded, a fact he kept brazenly quiet when agreeing to the job.

Another luxury was the array of cars he found before him in the garage beneath Maddox's penthouse in Las Vegas. In all the work he had done previously, he had had to purchase any cars he wanted to use. The black Audi e-tron GT he picked out wasn't particularly low-profile, but it was sleek and it was fast and it got him to Denver in Colorado by the early hours of the following morning.

He didn't stop to sleep before proceeding to the scrapyard on the outskirts of the city. When he arrived, he found it to be seemingly deserted, the gates closed and locked.

Stepping out of the car, Aurel traced the razor wire fence bounding the site and half an hour later found himself back where he started, having found no weak points to exploit. His next plan of action was much less subtle and he reached for a heavy pair of bolt cutters with which he began to work his way through the wire mesh comprising the gate.

He was contorting his body through the hole he had created when an old man thrust open the door to a ramshackle old bungalow situated at the edge of the yard.

"Hey!" the man rasped, hobbling down the patio steps and cocking an assault rifle. "Hey!"

Aurel had fired two shots from his Glock-34 before the man could raise the gun. He cried out as his prosthetic leg was shattered and he fell to his knees.

"Where is Vince Foster?" Aurel thrust the man to the ground and kneeled on his chest.

"I don't know what you're talking about!" the man spat defiantly. Aurel unloaded another round into his hand, mangling it beyond repair and evoking an ear-shattering scream which transcended the man's raspy voice.

"Do not lie to me. Where is Noah Cox's car?"

"He gave it to me to destroy," the man said between shallow, ragged breaths. "Don't know why! It's not my job to ask!"

"Where did he go?"

"I don't know, alright? Vince is a shrewd man. He doesn't let on any more than is absolutely necessary. And I've long since learned not to pry. Our relationship is one of business and business alone. And it involves a great deal of mutual respect. So you can waterboard me, smash my kneecap, rip off my nails, put me on a stretcher, whatever you damn well please! You won't be able to get any information that I don't have!"

Aurel pressed his knee further into the man's chest, forcing him to strain for breath. "You know something."

"Something useful to you? Fat chance. Who are you, anyways? Government? Not mine, judging by that accent of yours. What is it, Russian? Polish?"

"I will kill you if you do not tell me."

"Oh, I don't doubt it. I know how these things go. Do you want me to lie to you? Do you want me to send you on a goose chase after you've unloaded one last bullet into my head? I'll tell you exactly what happened last time I saw Vince Foster. He drove in with his partner and gave me the both of their cars to destroy. He kept the tracker from his—don't ask me why, he didn't tell me. Then they bought an old antique off me, one which hadn't been retrofitted with any modern tracker or internet box. Paid for in crypto. Drove off in it the same day, both of them. Is that satisfactory? Rip my damned chip out of my head if you want to verify it for yourself."

Aurel did just that before standing up and shooting him in the head.

He didn't have access to the facilities he needed to analyse the chip in the car or Maddox's penthouse and so found himself visiting a public library for the first time in his life. The contents of the chip were encrypted, but a scan of the old man's severed finger that Aurel had sawn off quickly bypassed that. That allowed him access to an expansive repository of more than ten years of constant footage, which he narrowed down to only the past few weeks before beginning to sift through at a hundred times the regular speed.

The old man's life was repetitive. That was Aurel's first judgement. Every day, he woke up and trudged around the scrapyard, never leaving the confines of the raggedy fence that surrounded it. He sat up and accelerated the footage to be even faster after realising the fence's shoddy condition, remembering how immaculate it had been when he had arrived earlier in the day. He continued to accelerate it until days passed in seconds, unable to discern the various faces of customers that arrived in all manner of exotic vehicles or the myriad jobs that occupied the scrapper's daily life.

He stopped only when he could see that the old fence had been torn down and in the frozen frame could see several workers in construction vehicles erecting the fence that existed in its current state. Winding back a few days, he finally spotted the vehicles he was looking for.

The old man rasped a command to open the gate for the monstrous F-150 and trailing Accord that waited patiently outside the disobedient mechanism. Aurel glanced askance at the portraits of Vince Foster and Noah Cox he had been provided by Maddox to match their identities with those who stepped out of the vehicles before spectating the arrangement of the destruction of said vehicles.

What then transpired was not something about which Aurel had been informed, as he watched the old man present to the two hitmen an antique car, allowing them to test drive it before Vince paid for it himself. The transaction encouraged Aurel to check his public financial records, and there was no mention of the two-hundred and fifty thousand dollar sum quoted by the scrapper. He also checked the scrapper's financial records, finding the transaction in his cryptocurrency wallet but coming from a wallet labelled as belonging to one Felix Weißmann. He traced the source of the money into that wallet, but it had been laundered well and he couldn't connect it to Vince.

"One more thing," Aurel then heard Vince say, as he grabbed the old man's shoulder. "The tracker on the F-150. Do you think I could take it with me?"

There wasn't much left to see in the footage after the old man handed Vince the tracker and watched him drive away in the Mazda. The vehicles were procedurally destroyed, the new fence was ordered, and then eventually Aurel watched himself arrive. It was at that point that he removed the chip from the library's reader and departed, making sure to deposit the severed finger in the nearest bin on his way out.

CHAPTER 19

Vince briskly departed the office, resuming his disguise and wasting no time in hailing a taxi to take him back to his house. When he arrived, he headed straight into the garage where his car had been returned by Maddox's men. Before settling into the driver's seat, he did a quick visual sweep around the exterior, falling to his hands and knees to inspect the car's underside. He found nothing, but his paranoia persisted. He proceeded to retrieve a radio frequency detector and swept the car once more. Signals could be detected from power-on, as would be expected. But the intensity of them increased greatly as he passed by the rear left wheel.

Reaching down, Vince pried the hubcap from the wheel, and it was there, attached to the centre of the rim, that he picked up a small, inconspicuous black device. As he held it closer to the frequency detector, it beeped faster and faster as if it were a Geiger counter and the black device a lump of uranium.

He walked out into the street and approached a van that had parked nearby, checking that nobody was watching, and then affixed the device to the vehicle's underside. He then proceeded back towards the garage.

"Vince?"

His disguise was inadequate in preventing well-known acquaintances from recognising him, as was proved when Ruth exited the building next door. She was visibly upset, though she tried to resolve herself as she spotted Vince and began to walk towards him.

"Hello, Ruth," he said amicably, though wishing she had never seen him. "Are you alright?"

"No, Vince, I'm not alright." Her makeshift resolve fell apart at once and tears welled in her eyes. "I'm fucking sick and tired of it. Noah's not a photographer, is he? And you're not his manager, are you?"

"Calm down," Vince said uneasily, slowly corralling her into his garage and closing the door. "What are you talking about?"

"Don't bullshit me," she snapped, sniffling. "I've put up with this charade for so long. Pretending that these weeks-long trips abroad were normal. Like they're part of any photographer's job. I'm not stupid, Vince. I've refused to get angry at Noah about this for so long because I've always imagined he must have the best of intentions to keep such a secret. But how long can I keep that up? How long can I sit there, going about my day-to-day life in the vague hope that my boyfriend returns one day? It's been months since you both left! And now you turn up on some random occasion without even letting me know? I want the truth, Vince! I deserve to know the truth!"

Vince waited a while to mull over his response before giving it. "Noah asked me to check in on you. I intended to do that after I'd finished my job."

"And what, exactly, is your job?"

"We've maintained a fake story for your protection, Ruth. My wife doesn't know what I really do and I've been at it for more than a decade. This is not a unique arrangement. Not only does it mean you don't become ensnared in our affairs, it also means you don't become a liability. We live in a dangerous world as it is. And the world we— Noah and I—work in is even more so. Hence why, on paper, I am a freelance security consultant. And why Noah is a photographer."

"Security consultant," Ruth echoed.

"You can infer from that what you will. But I'm sorry, I cannot tell you what I do. I can't tell anyone."

"You can fucking well tell the people you're closest to. You haven't told your wife what you do but you hate your wife, Vince. There's where the difference lies. Noah doesn't hate me. And I don't hate him. The bedrock of any relationship is unabating trust. It's a trust you and Noah share but I've been unable to build myself. And it destroys me. I sit there some nights, awake in my bed, wondering what I do wrong. What it is that means you have earned the trust of the person I love but I haven't. How is that fair?"

"You do have Noah's trust," Vince reassured her coolly. "And you have mine. But the problem is that knowledge is dangerous. There exist people in our spheres who would target you to get at us. And if you knew who we were, who we really were, then you would be a danger to us. But when we leave you in the dark, it keeps us safe and it makes you, as a target, worthless. Do you understand this? Noah doesn't keep his secret from you out of a lack of trust but because he wants to keep you safe. He would never want to jeopardise you and takes heart-wrenching measures to be sure of that."

Ruth's lip quivered and then she fell into sobbing. Vince gingerly accepted her onto his shoulder and they remained that way for several minutes as Ruth expunged her body of all the tears it could muster.

"It's not a way to live," she finally choked, her words barely audible, muffled by Vince's coat. "Put yourself in my shoes. Would you be able to put up with it? Would you resist the temptation to just leave it all behind and find someone who can tell you the truth? Who can be their actual self at all times?"

Vince decided to keep his truthful response to himself. "Noah's coming home soon. In the meantime, I need to go."

"Where are you going?"

"You know I can't tell you."

"You could at least tell me something. Some lie, like the two of you have always done. At least I'd have some semblance of comfort. I know I've just spent the past ten minutes complaining about that, but what else do I have, Vince? What am I meant to cling onto?"

"Goodbye, Ruth. It'll be alright."

CHAPTER 20

Aurel didn't bother to sleep before setting off to Omaha, instead restimulating his brain with his neural chip. He knew the dangers associated with that but felt unyieldingly determined to prove to Maddox that he could do the job effectively. Above all, he wanted to make a name for himself, and he knew this was the greatest opportunity he would ever receive.

He didn't stop to eat at any point, instead heading straight to the GPS location of the tracker which should have been affixed to the destroyed F-150. It was found instead attached to the underside of a Chevrolet SUV several floors up a multistorey car park in the city centre. He ripped the device from the car's chassis with a grunt and left in search of a hotel where he finally gave in to his body's needs. He woke up early the next morning and, before resuming his hunt, found a table at a diner from which he could call Maddox. The response was almost immediate, startlingly so, though Aurel maintained his steadfast neutrality.

"AK. Have you found him?"

"No. I followed the tracker to a false car."

"I thought as much. We followed the tracker on his car but he found that one, too. Had stuck it to the underside of a van. Where are you right now?"

Aurel scowled before replying, "Omaha."

"Did you go to the scrapyard? What happened there?"

"A man there sold Vince a new car. Destroyed the old one and Noah Cox's. He used a fake identity to make the payment. Felix Weißmann."

"That's good, actually. Did you get any identities that Noah was using?"

"No."

"Whatever, I can still cobble something together. I'll get in touch with my American contact and they'll be able to check flight records. We'll hopefully be able to work out whether Noah and Vince came to London together or if he's struck out on his own. Another thing, while you're in Omaha. Taylor Carrillo, the senator, his truck was found out in the woods near where you are. And I've just got this feeling in my gut that something isn't quite as it seems. I have no proof to back that up, but my American contact has access to traffic data and public footage so I can send it to you and you can have a look. Maybe find something out. This is relevant, mind you, because it was Vince and Noah who made him disappear."

"Okay," Aurel grunted. "I also need data from Vince's new car. It's a Mazda from 1993. English import. L010 WHU."

"Alright. Anything else?"

"No. I'll get to work."

Aurel was the one to put down the phone as a waitress came to take his order. Through a strained conversation in which she routinely stumbled over herself in an attempt to understand his accent, Aurel finally managed to order something to eat and drink while he waited patiently for the information to come through from Maddox.

When it arrived, it was at once. There were no dribs and drabs—rather, Aurel found himself inundated with entire databases of traffic records for the entire city of Omaha on the day of Senator Carrillo's disappearance, a full list of all flights made to and from American airports under the name Felix Weißmann, and any instances of number plate recognition for Vince's Mazda as well as Taylor Carrillo's pickup truck.

It didn't take long to find something of interest. Aurel centred his focus initially on Senator Carrillo, reviewing snippets of CCTV footage of his truck as it had been captured around the city. The view into the driver's seat of the car wasn't particularly clear, though he could make out two individuals whose ethnicities he could at least match to Vince and Noah. The time spent driving wasn't of much value, but he kept watching, and eventually was rewarded when they pulled up in front of a hotel and one of the individuals, his face shrouded in dark sunglasses and a mask, stepped out while the other idled in the truck outside. Though facial recognition was unable to assign an identity, the bulk of his features matched that of Vince Foster and he could only assume that the person with him was Noah Cox.

The man looked as though he was moving into the building and then the footage cut out, freezing on a single frame where Aurel could just make out the discreet shape of a small device tucked into Vince's hand. Fast-forwarding through more of the footage revealed it to remain that way until several hours later, when the truck had disappeared and there was no sign of Vince, Noah, or Carrillo.

He cursed and checked for further instances of number plate recognition on the pickup, only to plot a steady string of coordinates leading out of the city and to the location where it had been found. Cursing, he shut down the laptop and bundled into his car in search of a more physical pursuit.

There was no car park at the hotel and so he pulled over to the very spot where Vince and Noah had parked in the footage. He felt no need to shroud his identity as he strode inside, eyes set on the reception counter occupied by what he could only have described as a teenager with very little interest in acknowledgement of his approach.

"Hello," Aurel eventually said, the teenager finally lifting his head from his phone. "I am looking for someone."

"Oh yeah?" the teenager replied. His eyes then fell straight back to his phone.

Aurel reached forward and grabbed him by the scruff of his neck, wrenching him out of his chair to bring their faces together. The device fell from his hands and clattered against the desk as he was held firmly in the air before the expressionless hitman, who reached a hand up to feel around his head for a neural chip, which he promptly ejected upon finding.

A door behind the desk swung open and Aurel reached his free hand down to his hip, unholstering and pointing his Glock at the man who appeared unassumingly in the doorway. His hands rose immediately to the sides of his head and he remained stationary in what seemed to be a rehearsed fashion.

"You." He gestured with his gun to the now vacant chair. "Sit."

The man in the doorway acted as instructed as Aurel thrust the receptionist onto the table and fished through his pocket for a handful of cable ties. He dragged the teenager down onto the floor and bound his hands to the other man before sauntering over to the entrance and twisting the lock.

"Someone was here not long ago," Aurel began. "A man named Vince Foster. He may have told you his name was Felix Weißmann. Tell me what you know about this man. Either of you."

"I don't know what the hell you're talking about," the older man, who Aurel assumed must have been the manager, responded first. "I ain't never heard either of those names in my life."

"He was here three days ago."

"Look, we'd love to help you if it means getting out of this situation, but we really cannot. You've given us a name, one that neither of us recognise. What's this guy look like? Help us out."

"Dark brown hair. Dark clothes. He wears a mask and sunglasses to cover his face," Aurel supplied.

"Are you talking about the server guy?" the receptionist chimed in from the floor. "He wasn't called Vince or Felix. What was it?"

"First name started with an R, if I remember correctly," the manager said. "Can't remember it for the life of me, but his surname was Quinn. Mr Quinn. But I guess you don't have that name?"

"What do you mean, server guy?" He directed his attention to the teenager.

"Server guy. He came in, did his whole salesman spiel, and we agreed on a pretty cosy deal. He's hosting our server on the cloud."

"What did he do while he was here? What did you say to him other than arranging business?"

"Not a whole lot," the manager replied. "He just fiddled around with the server and then left. Said he'd be back later. Who is this guy? What'd he do to you?"

Aurel's attention fell again to the receptionist, whose face reflected deep thought. "You. What did he say to you?"

"It's not so much what he said," the teenager said, creasing his forehead. "It's what he did. He just unplugged the cameras and then he disappeared off somewhere. Five minutes after that, he left."

"And he came alone?"

"Yeah. I didn't see anyone else come in."

"Do you have any security footage?"

"I would show you, but, you know."

Aurel revealed a pair of wire cutters from the pocket of his trench coat and freed the receptionist, though his gun remained trained on his head for the entire duration of the time he spent poring through the computer for the stored footage. The hitman paid attention to the timestamps in the top corner of the screen, the receptionist jabbering on about something he wasn't really listening to.

"Stop there," he suddenly said, causing the teenager to almost jump in surprise. "Zoom in on the door."

The camera enhanced to display in greater clarity the thinly visible view into the street outside. Panning back and forth between the split shards of footage, he asked to raise the volume and held his ear closely to the computer's speakers.

"Listen," he said. "The engine idling."

Distinctly audible in the former section of the footage was a low synthetic rumbling as would have been made by an idling pre-war vehicle. Such a modification was not un-common, especially amongst those with larger cars and trucks. In the next section of footage, though, the sound had cut out.

"Whoever was idling in the car got out," Aurel declared. "They came into the building. That's why Vince killed the cameras. Close this. I need a guestlist. Everyone staying in the hotel right now."

The receptionist quickly set about bringing up a database housing the details of every single active booking, with names, durations, room numbers and everything. It was at this point that Aurel took over, grasping the teenager's hands together and holding them behind his back as he did so. There weren't many bookings, so it didn't take him a very long time to find that for which he was looking.

"I need a key card. Room thirty-one."

"All the spares are in that drawer there."

He opened the desk drawer gestured to by the receptionist and retrieved the card in a plastic sleeve labelled *3.31* before revealing another cable tie. He then returned the receptionist to his original position at the base of the chair and stormed upstairs, screwing a silencer onto the end of his pistol.

As he came to the third floor, he quieted his footsteps and paced gingerly towards the door adorned with the number thirty-one. Stopping outside, careful not to transgress the view of the peephole, Aurel listened intently through the hotel's poorly insulated walls for sounds of activity. The only speech came from neighbouring rooms, only silence to be discerned from that booked by Felix Weißmann and Matteo Schulz. He pivoted to the other side of the door, bracing his pistol in his right hand and grasping the key card in his left.

He swiped to unlock the door and had made his way into the room before the man inside had time to even raise himself from the bed. It wasn't Vince Foster or Noah Cox, but it was almost as much of a reward.

"Eject your chip or I will kill you now," Aurel said sternly but quietly, the door falling shut behind him as the man on the bed raised his arms in surrender.

"Easy," the man, easily identifiable in the shafts of morning light as Senator Taylor Carrillo, cautioned. "I don't have a chip. Never have."

"Where is Vince Foster?"

"I don't know who that is."

"And Noah Cox?"

"Likewise."

The Senator wasn't ready for the blow and almost fell to the floor, struggling to recuperate himself, thoroughly unprepared for the subsequent blow that followed. Blood jetted from his mouth and spattered across the musty window as Aurel grabbed him and smashed his head against the dim lamp sitting atop the rickety bedside table, shattering it entirely and making far more noise than he would have liked.

"I know you are lying so you can continue like this and prolong your suffering or you can give them up and I won't have to spend hours torturing you."

Before the senator could respond, Aurel unveiled a wickedly sharp Bowie knife and plunged it into Carrillo's gut, reaching forward to cover his face with his hand as he attempted to scream but managing only a muffled whine.

"Where are they?" Aurel whispered directly into his ear as he gently released his hand from the senator's mouth.

"I don't know. I haven't talked to them for a few days. Either of them."

"Bullshit."

He covered Carrillo's mouth again and grabbed the knife before twisting it, his hand vibrating with the scream that tried to fracture the air.

"Where are they?"

"I... don't... know..."

"I've already mangled your intestines. If you tell me where they've gone, you might be able to get to the hospital in time to avoid sepsis. But every second counts. I ask again. Where are they?"

The senator winced and took slow, heavy breaths, sweat beading on his forehead and pooling under his arms. Each of his words were spoken slowly and with great delay in between. "I... don't... know."

Through his stupor, Carrillo looked longingly to his left and Aurel traced his gaze to the closed room door. "Is that it? Are you expecting someone?"

"I... don't... know..."

Aurel retrieved yet another cable tie and ordered Carrillo to extend his hands. He tied them together and then bound them above his head to the bedframe before unlocking his phone and dialling Maddox with a knowing sense of urgency.

As before, Maddox answered with matching urgency. "What is it now, AK? Are you going to do any work yourself?"

"I have found Senator Carrillo," Aurel said, ignoring the oligarch's snide remark. "He is alone and has given me what I want. What do you want me to do with him?"

Maddox chuckled over the other end of the phone before responding. "Oh, you are good. How much do you want for it?"

"Consider it collateral damage. Am I to proceed?"

"Wait, wait, wait, I want to see this. I'm going to call you on your chip." The connection dropped and then promptly resumed, this time between the pair's neural chips, and Aurel allowed Maddox to see through his eyes. "Oh, let me speak to him, too, would you?"

Aurel triggered a setting which filtered Maddox's voice through a miniscule pair of speakers implemented into his shoulders. "Good afternoon, Taylor," the oligarch said with palpable joy. "Oh, you aren't a pretty sight."

Carrillo grimaced and spat blood over the yellowed carpet. "Go fuck yourself."

"So irate. How did you manage to convince Vince not to kill you, Taylor? For future reference."

"I told him... the truth. Something you... ought to learn to do... sometimes. Keep betraying your allies... and... it'll bite you in the ass... one day. Mark my words."

"Sure it will. Okay, I'm bored now. AK, do your thing. Wait, actually." Maddox then imitated the voice of Grand Moff Tarkin as he said, "You may fire when ready."

The oligarch erupted with laughter as the bullet tore through Carrillo's skull.

CHAPTER 21

It was easy to cross into the United Republic of England and Wales. The government there encouraged the inward movement of Londoners in the hopes that it would stimulate their stagnant economy. They even turned a blind eye to the rampant bribery committed by said Londoners as they trafficked drugs, weapons, illicit money, and people across the border. The system in place may as well have been official. Vince pulled up to the inspection, showed the guards his pistol, and they named a price. He paid it and drove away without hassle.

Although Vince had been born in London while it was still the capital of what was then the United Kingdom, he did not identify himself as anything other than a Londoner. Even to that title he felt no powerful affiliation. But he found it less embarrassing than to associate with the dilapidated nation he found himself driving through. One which had once been so great, but now lay in a permanent state of stagnation and disrepair.

Blenheim Palace remained majestic despite the dreary grey blanketing the sky. Vince had been before, as a child, on a sunnier day. Of course, then he was able to freely traverse the grounds. Now, the gates were shut, and he only caught a fleeting glance as he drove along the adjacent main road in search of a location from which he could covertly begin his reconnaissance.

He found parking in the neighbouring town of Woodstock, an arrangement of stone houses several hundred years old which blended into the clouds above and through their monotonous beauty somehow evoked an unsettling melancholy.

There weren't many people around, but those that were bore expressions accentuating this very inexplicable emotion with which Vince found himself suddenly awash. He shook his head as if to physically disperse the sensation and meandered to the back of his car where he retrieved a drone from the boot and set about activating it and letting it into the air.

He sat back into the driver's seat and tuned into the drone's controls through his neural chip, hoping dearly that any security forces guarding the oligarch's grounds wouldn't be spooked by it. The devices that were so commonplace in the world's metropolises were utterly absent in the English countryside, and the model Vince operated was by no means inconspicuous.

Lifting up into the air over the empty town, Vince navigated the drone around the northern end of the estate and over the river before heading south towards a dense patch of trees. He dropped towards the ground and used the estate's sprawling gardens to stay as concealed as he possibly could in his approach to the mansion.

He failed almost immediately in his attempt to remain unnoticed. Several gardeners milling about the intertwining gravel pathways spotted the sizable drone as it progressed through the grounds, chatting unsurely to one another. Vince accelerated the drone and abandoned stealth as he soared up and into an open window, only fitting with a few centimetres to spare.

The person occupying the room was a half-dressed Christie West, owner of the estate and one of the less prominent—but still influential—London oligarchs. She screamed as the drone blitzed through the open curtains and reached for bedsheets with which to conceal herself. Vince cursed in his head and reversed back out of the window, soaring around the upper levels of the mansion's exterior in an attempt to find another open window.

He checked the camera situated on the drone's underside to find that several members of the estate's security personnel had filed into the open and were aiming weapons at the drone. Bullets subsequently whistled past and Vince accelerated the drone to its maximum speed, a setting which also made the device terribly difficult to manoeuvre.

As the bullets continued to sail past in reams, Vince diverged from his tactic of speed and instead moved towards the building and hugged the wall as closely as was possible without the drone's blades grinding against the stone. As he had predicted, the assault ceased and the security below regrouped the discuss a new plan.

He found another open window as he continued to traverse the mansion's vast exterior and leisurely lowered the drone through it. Inside was another bedroom, occupied by a cleaner sweeping the floors. They eyed the drone suspiciously and took weary steps towards the open door, but Vince got there first.

Finally, he had access to the building's main body and he set about mapping it with speed. Through English Baroque corridors, halls, and a formidable portion of the hundred and eighty-seven rooms he manoeuvred, some left untouched by the new occupier and some renovated entirely. Security stormed through the building as Vince continued to have his way and the two opposing sides soon came face-to-face—except this time, Vince had nowhere to go, and the security forces were preparedly well equipped.

One of them held up a small grey device from which Vince could see several protruding antennae and upon activating it, Vince's connection became jerky and unstable. He quickly attempted to shift to another frequency but found that all he tried were congested with the same insurmountable noise and he soon lost connection with the drone entirely.

The hitman tuned out of the neural chip feed and took a moment to overcome the expected wave of nausea. He then promptly ignited the car and drove away, travelling west with no real aim as to his final destination. He only wanted to escape as far from detection as possible.

He wasn't worried about the drone being traceable to him. He had erased the serial numbers from it and all the parts inside it after buying it. He had also removed the internal storage from the device and made it so that all camera feed was streamed to and stored in his chip alone. His foray into the depths of the English Southwest wasn't wholly necessary, but he had time to kill and didn't want to risk travel back into London where he now knew that Maddox's agents were tracking him.

One of the first things he did upon arriving to a suitably quiet town in which to wait until Friday was purchase an inflatable kayak. After that, his waking hours comprised sitting in a hotel room and gleaning as much information as he could acquire about the gathering.

From what he had found, it seemed that Christie had invited near every oligarch in London, of which there were thirty-two—one for each borough in theory, though the actual practice of division of authority was much more blurred. They in turn were bringing whole reams of staff and vaguely connected business colleagues while Christie herself had paid for security—but, Vince thought, not nearly enough for the scale of the event. Whether that was out of frugality or arrogance he couldn't discern, as exact details to the gathering's amenities were few and far between.

Vince. Problem.

The message from Noah came through the day before the soirée as Vince was retrieving his dinner from the delivery drone. He called his friend without hesitation.

Noah picked up straight away, but Vince was first to speak. "What's happened?"

"Carrillo isn't responding to the code I set for him. And the police were called to the hotel while I was out today."

"He's dead?"

"It would appear that way. I do apologise, Vince. It was poor timing. Whoever killed him, they did it at the one moment I wasn't there to catch them."

"What do you mean, whoever killed him? Why haven't you been looking out for something like this to happen?"

"Mate, I have. Have a bit of faith. I don't think this was premeditated, and I also don't think they were after Carrillo. If anything, I think they were after me and you."

"And what makes you so convinced of that?"

"Because I spoke to the FBI and submitted to their investigation. Their forensics guys recovered footage from the hotel CCTV. This guy was an amateur, didn't even delete it, just pulled the plug and shot the camera. Heard the attacker mention one Felix Weißmann before stealing the key card to room thirty-one on the third floor. Oh, that's right. The attacker killed the hotel owner and the kid on his way out. They don't care about mess. They left plenty of it."

"Did they identify the attacker?"

"Not yet. No facial recognition hits in the Americans' database. He looks and sounds Slavic, so contact has been made with the Europeans, but nothing has been heard back yet."

"Has to be Maddox. It's good news, if anything, because it means he's not on to us just yet. But... how long will that last?"

"Well I checked around. He's not here. And there's more—he killed Leo, too. Police are yet to find that. I don't trust Leo not to have spilled beforehand."

"Nor me. But what information could he have found if he's killed all the people he got it from? And then just disappeared?"

Noah hesitated. "Maybe he hasn't disappeared."

CHAPTER 22

Thirty minutes passed and it was at that point that Aurel understood something to be amiss.

He decisively holstered the weapon he had held all the while, his arm numb with fatigue, and moved into the room's entryway to peer through the peephole. He saw nothing and cautiously waved a hand over the sensor to open the door before retreating, waiting, and then proceeding again.

The corridor was empty and silent. The arrangement of muffled sounds he had observed upon first arrival had dissipated entirely, and he felt a distinct lack of control as he trudged down the stairs, each footstep invoking a groan from the carpeted floorboards. His hand hovered over the holstered Glock as he progressed downwards.

On the floor above the ground, the blanketing silence was finally interrupted. Not by voices, but by a crescendo of distant sirens rolling towards the hotel. Aurel unholstered his gun and ran downstairs.

Noah Cox was not waiting for him, as he had feared. Instead, a woman stood next to the hotel manager and the receptionist, who both stood free. They all cast horrified gazes upon the Slovak as he made his reappearance and rose their hands in meek protest at the summary execution they could have done nothing to prevent.

Over the chorus of sirens, Aurel fired a round into the lobby's single CCTV camera and then moved further into the office behind the front desk. He found the outlet for the server and pulled it, frustratedly aware of the fact that much more needed to be done to wipe the evidence of his presence but accepting of the imminent arrival of the police. Under the circumstances, he chose to flee.

The first police cars arrived as he practically fell into the driver's seat and jetted into the steady stream of traffic to the loud fury of the motorists comprising said traffic. The police didn't even attempt to follow him, the two cars that had turned up both stopping outside the hotel and allowing Aurel to slip away.

He didn't drive far. He found parking in a high-rise a couple blocks over and then, donning a mask, walked back in the direction of the hotel.

Two police cars had multiplied into a squadron, a strobing red-blue lightshow showering the dreary urban façade with colour. Officers conversed with paramedics and investigators as they all arrived in turn, the corpses of those

Aurel had killed wheeled out of the building in body bags. The Slovak maintained his distance, joining the crowd of other nosy bystanders. Many of them recorded the affair with their phones, or, in the case of the visibly more affluent, with their neural chips.

Before long, the scene was flooded by local news anchors. The story, as it seemed, wasn't big enough for national news, but reporters and drones from seemingly every news outlet in Nebraska descended upon the emergency responders with little regard for the disruption it caused. Some tried to force their way into the building, at which point the police responded with a show of brutality, discharging a bullet into the nearest news drone and then kicking the wreckage towards the remaining reporters. From that point onwards, they kept their distance.

Hotel guests soon began to leave the building with police escorts as the entire building was cordoned off. The situation remained mostly stagnant as the gears of bureaucracy turned. The media grew bored of the lack of development, as exhibited by the departure of their drones and then their reporters. And then the FBI arrived and the falloff in interest was immediately reversed.

It didn't take long for the news to leak that Senator Carrillo's body had been found inside and the few reporters who had remained on the scene rejoiced. Soon enough, the conference of journalists and cameras that had occupied the road beforehand returned at twice the size. The story which only five minutes beforehand would have maybe cracked the front page of state-level papers had suddenly turned into a new development to one of the leading national investigations.

Aurel didn't move all the while. He kept a sharp eye on the doorway as it was increasingly obscured by individuals and vans the size of small tanks, and finally spotted what he was hoping for. Engaged in dialogue with two of the officers from the FBI stood Noah Cox, his mouth covered by a mask and his words indiscernible through the impassable cacophony. A well-aimed shot through the crowd and Aurel could have claimed his reward. There were enough people around to flee with relative ease. But there was also far too much risk, and he didn't feel confident enough to accurately hit a shot that far with only a pistol. So instead, he continued to watch.

Law enforcement and journalists and bystanders were joined by politicians and more journalists and more cameras. Statements were given by every party. Aurel retreated into a café with a view over the affair as the FBI began to move towards the pedestrians, questioning them each in turn as witnesses. The Slovak sipped an ersatz coffee with a bitter expression.

He stayed there for a while, just as the crowd remained unmoving in front of the hotel. His eyes never fell from Noah Cox, who continued to engage with the officers handling the scene for far longer than was, Aurel thought, expectable for a man whose job involved profound breach of the law. Of course, the officers probably didn't know who he was.

"Excuse me, honey?" Perhaps an hour had passed when Aurel's focus was interrupted by the café's single waitress.

"Were you gonna order anythin' else? We don't have many seats, is all."

He turned from the window to set eyes upon the waitress, quickly flitted his eyes back to Noah, and then turned again. "Coffee. Black."

"Any food? You must be hungry, been sat there a while."

"No."

Aurel found a ten-dollar bill and placed it on the table, sliding it towards the waitress who accepted it uneasily before disappearing back behind the counter. It took him a few moments to readjust to the minute changes in the scene as he resumed his surveillance. He found Noah just as he exited the zone that had been cordoned off, his mouth moving as if engaged in conversation as he walked along the street alone. He rounded the corner, and it was at that point that Aurel stood up and departed, the waitress arriving with his coffee to an empty table.

He kept his head low and his pace quick, hugging the sides of buildings and choosing a route which passed by the most cover in the form of dilapidated bus shelters and luminescent advertising boards and great concrete pillars. Traffic along the street had ground to a halt with half of the road blocked off and veritable battalions of oversized American cars made Aurel's undetected flight far easier than he had expected.

He crossed the street at the intersection where Noah had disappeared and turned his fast walk into a jog. Effective cover remained paramount, with Noah casting an apprehensive glance over his shoulder at regular intervals. He didn't appear to be speaking anymore, and moved with longer strides at a greater pace. Aurel felt imbued with adrenaline, his Glock suddenly heavy in its holster, his arm electrically anxious to draw it.

Noah then stopped and Aurel fell into a nearby alleyway. He remained stationary for some time before a taxi rolled up to stop beside him. The hitman stepped into it and it rolled away.

The Slovak cursed in his mother tongue and burst out of his cover. He stepped into the way of oncoming traffic, prompting the furious blaring of several horns and the angry denunciation from the driver of the car directly before him. Stepping around to the side of the car, he yanked the door open, grasping the driver's shirt and tearing him from the seat. He hadn't intended to kill him, but the driver pulled a gun on him, so he had to act first.

The benefit of that was that it ensured he wouldn't open his phone and remotely disable the car. A vigilante in a trailing pickup stepped down from the cockpit of their vehicle with a pistol of their own and Aurel shot them, too, before sliding into the seat of the hijacked vehicle and slamming on the accelerator. The door slammed shut with the sudden jerk of force though the generated traffic jam remained, as many of the drivers had run screaming from their cars during the affair.

Noah had a head start of perhaps thirty seconds. Aurel tuned into his neural chip and enabled his head-up display, enabling a widget which highlighted a given number plate. He fed in the plate of the taxi that Noah had entered and swept his eyes across the traffic ahead as he surged forwards through the space he had created with the hijacking, hoping eagerly for a hit.

It wasn't long until he found himself followed by sirens, the arrival of two police cars from opposing streets coinciding with the fluorescent blue light that traced itself around the registration plate of a car in the right lane almost fifty metres ahead. Aurel sped through the little available space to catch up with the taxi as it rolled to a stop at an intersection, the traffic lights turning green as he arrived alongside it.

He yanked the wheel hard, locking it to the right and pressing his foot to the floor. The car launched into the other and they both spun out onto the side of the row, flattening a row of blooming flowers, decimating a streetlight, and almost bowling over a cluster of pedestrians who leapt out of the way with moments to spare. Sirens blared as the police coerced their way through the growing throng of traffic. Aurel thrust open his door only for it to collide with another streetlight, one which remained standing, and wrenched himself out of the gap. His heart pounded. He stumbled onto the pavement, eyes narrowed as the first gunshot rang out.

Noah had escaped first; he took shelter behind the car in much the same way as Aurel did behind his own, crawling along the floor and unholstering his Glock. He peeked his head up only momentarily as the police began to bark orders over megaphones and another bullet whizzed past, shattering the windscreen and showering him in thousands of shards of glass.

"Put the weapons down!" The demand was not limited to Aurel, and the police had exited their vehicles behind Noah. "Drop them!"

The Slovak raised his gun over the bonnet of the car and unleashed a barrage of indiscriminate pot-shots at the car behind which he knew Noah Cox was taking shelter. The bullets pinged ineffectively off the metallic surface and Noah revealed himself at the other end of the vehicle to fire back in retaliation. Aurel ducked, the bullets passing over his head as the police officers issued their final warnings.

"Drop your weapons! Hands where I can see them!"

Aurel peered through the shattered remains of the hijacked car's window and saw both officers with their weapons trained upon an invisible Noah Cox. He slithered back through the uncomfortably tight gap into the driver's seat, conscious to keep his head lowered, and turned the car on. Several warning lights flashed up, alerting any driver focused on them to the damage amassed to the battered chassis and more critical parts. Aurel wasn't paying attention to that. His eyes didn't stray from the window.

Time seemed to move very slowly in the moments that followed. Aurel found himself engaged in a very high-stakes game of chicken, and from his new position within the car, he had no idea as to Noah's location. The droning hum of urbanity fell mute, the pounding of blood in his ears overwhelming his focus as he acted out the motions demanded by unadulterated adrenaline.

The first gunshot set off a chain reaction splitting the air like a series of firecrackers. Noah stood up in synchronicity with Aurel raising his head above the confines of the car's outer shell and they both locked eyes before unleashing a volley of bullets upon each other. The Slovak felt one pierce his shoulder as Noah was knocked backwards with the force of an impact and then both hitmen were showered by a further round of bullets from the police officers. Falling into the deepest recesses of the driver's seat, Aurel jerked the wheel to screeching protest from his shoulder and accelerated back into the road as more and more projectiles eviscerated what was left of the rear windscreen and peppered the crippled chassis with scores of holes. The onslaught didn't cease as he drove away, but its effectiveness certainly waned.

"Car. Get me directions to the car park on sixteenth street," Aurel barked, swerving precariously into and out of traffic. A sequence of arrows rapidly assembled and a crackly voice from a damaged speaker system began to issue directions to the street on which Aurel hoped to find safe refuge in the form of his own car. Those instructions battled against verbal warnings about the accrued damage and expected breakdown as he careened unrestrainedly towards the visible car park entrance.

He turned the wheel once more and was met with a reverberating bang as one of the front tyres burst. The car spiralled out of control and crashed into the barrier at the entrance, a jet of pain shooting down Aurel's arm with the force of collision. It didn't slow him down, as he left the car to an orchestra of arriving sirens.

More bullets grazed the pavement beneath his feet as he practically fell down the ramp into the car park. He regained his composure and sprinted to the stairs at the side of the room, bounding up them three at a time until he came to the floor on which he had parked the Audi.

Shouts echoed through the airy complex from every direction, each step the Slovak took pulsing new pain through his entire person. His car lit up in anticipation of his approach, the driver's door opening in coordination with a command he issued through his neural chip. He dived into the seat with complete disregard for the lodged bullet in his shoulder and slammed the door shut with so much force that he worried he could have broken it.

He gripped the wheel and rubber screeched against the concrete floor as he launched out of the space, following signs pointing to the exit at four times the indicated maximum speed.

The police that were chasing Aurel hadn't anticipated that he would have been in a vehicle. Turning a corner, one lone officer didn't even have time to draw his weapon before the Slovak collided with him. His body flew over the bonnet, crashing into the windscreen, shattering it, and continuing on to roll over the roof.

Despite the network of cracks obscuring his view, Aurel powered on. Down and down he drove, the police unable to stop him as he made his way closer and closer to the exit, where he finally burst onto the street. The police, all stationary around the crashed car at the entrance, weren't prepared to follow as he shot away at speed.

"Maddox," the Slovak grunted as a call he made was answered. "I need a doctor. And a mechanic."

CHAPTER 23

Noah stumbled backwards as the bullet tore into his chest. And then he fell forwards as the next three tore into his back.

He wasn't paying much attention to his assailant's escape. The vignette encapsulating his vision as he bled out on the ground was much more engrossing. He didn't resist as the police officers who had shot him turned him over, and he didn't really feel any pain as he died.

CHAPTER 24

When Vince lost connection with Noah, it took him all of five minutes to abandon his hiding and book a flight to Omaha.

The pit that formed in his stomach was consuming and encompassing. The void he felt left no room for other thought. He was lost in a dangerous concoction of guilt and sorrow and anger and despair.

The proportions of each emotion in the formulation were not static but changing with each passing moment. Initially, Vince found himself racked with guilt, unsure of how to deliver the news to a Ruth whom he had not even a week ago given his assurances. Guilt born of the fact that he was the one who had assigned Noah to watch over Carrillo, leaving him alone in a city to which he had never been. Guilt that he himself had survived.

And then, perhaps an hour into his drive back to London, he found sorrow and despair to be the dominating components in about equal measure. The more he thought about anything, the lower he felt. So he attempted to focus only on the road ahead, a strategy which seemed to work, if the goal was to feel nothing at all.

It wasn't in Vince's nature to feel so permanently distraught, and it didn't take long for anger to flush out everything else. It was an anger that snapped him back into focus, returning him from conscious absence. An anger that didn't control him, but fuelled him with raw passion and intensity.

He parked his car back in his own garage in London and took a helitaxi to the airport, too caught up in his rage to be wary of the danger he knew was present. In fact, part of him wanted Maddox to know where he was. Under normal circumstances, he wouldn't have given any of his enemies such an opportunity to prepare, but this time was different. He found himself against an enemy defined by confidence. Not unfounded, by any means, but the line between confident and cocky was thin and it was one to the contemptible side of which Maddox had long since crossed. It meant that Vince, too, could feel confident in his brazen act of defiance at the oligarch's sweeping control over one of the richest regions in the world.

His suspicions were affirmed when the helitaxi began to descend towards a clearing in the borough of Hounslow before they had arrived at the airport. Vince drew his gun and was moments from shooting the driver before he realised that the driver himself had lost control of the vehicle. The expression on his face could have been theatre, but to Vince it felt real, and he had no issue believing that Maddox's forces were able to remotely hijack individual vehicles within the interconnected system.

A squad of outfitted mercenaries awaited them in a park on the ground but Vince wasn't prepared to allow himself to be captured. The handles to open the doors were locked while in flight, but the windows were fallible to a single bullet. He found the emergency parachute beneath his seat and unloaded a round into the window on the right-hand side, shattering it and climbing out to cling precariously to the frame of the rapidly descending taxi. Manoeuvring into a position so that he was effectively crouched against the side of the vehicle, hands strained to hold on to the landing skids, he closed his eyes and then launched himself sideways and downwards.

The blades thundered past and were only centimetres from mincing him mid-air. He felt very slow as he watched the helitaxi continue to fall at a much faster rate than he now did, though the ground looked much larger as he viewed it through open sky as opposed to rounded glass windows.

His eyes fell upon the mercenaries who had watched the entire affair and were now scrambling to react to the development. Vince watched one of them retrieve what looked, from the distance, like a sniper rifle from the back of an SUV. The explosion of the weapon's discharge was mostly inaudible to Vince, his ears dominated by the whipping of the wind as he fell. Though each shot became louder and louder as the hitman fell closer and closer to the ground, beyond the distance at which he would have liked to have safely activated the parachute. But he knew that he would die the moment he pulled the cord if there was nothing between him and his would-be assassin.

Hounslow wasn't a particularly vertical region. It hadn't seen much of the rapid development pioneered in the post-independence city centre, probably owing to the fact that it was home to Heathrow Airport. While the skyline of Westminster reflected that of Manhattan in its sweeping amalgamation of skyscrapers and vanity projects, Hounslow remained a snapshot of a time long since passed. It made it very difficult to time the deployment of a parachute so as not to collide with the earth at two hundred and fifty kilometres per hour while avoiding being picked out of the air like a clay pigeon.

The town centre, the sprawling suburbs, and the patches of greenery in the sparsely located parks all came hurtling towards Vince at what felt like an accelerating pace. More gunshots rang out, a few of them passing him by closely enough that he heard their taunting hiss as they flew. He had maybe five seconds before deployment wouldn't have saved him, and so he counted those five seconds before pulling the cord and letting loose the expansive red fabric.

Another round was loosed from the sniper and this time it found a target, though that target was Vince's parachute instead of Vince. A hole that could only have been the

work of a .50 calibre appeared above him and was joined
shortly thereafter by another as he floated down towards
the centre of a busy road in the town centre.

The fury of British motorists fell upon him unmoderated
as the road was shrouded in the shadow of the descending
parachute. Nearby police officers looked upon the specta-
cle with bewilderment as the assassin took one final shot,
the bullet missing its mark by mere centimetres as it instead sliced through the mechanisms holding together the
ropes above Vince's head. He fell to one side as the parachute swayed and then caught the tops of lampposts and
balconies. His landing was not graceful but the hitman
managed to wrench his way out of the entangling contrap-
tion as a torrent of verbal abuse struck him like a shockwave. That was simple enough to ignore, but the pair of
police officers who approached him from the pavement
were not so easily disregarded.

"Hello," the first of them, a middle-aged woman with
greying hair, began politely. "What's happened here,
then?"

"Helitaxi emergency," Vince responded abruptly, not
even meeting her gaze as he brushed the dust from his
coat and trousers. "There's a band of gunmen in the park
just across the way. You want to go talk to them, not me."

"We'll dispatch someone to have a look." She moved to
stand in Vince's way as he tried to leave the scene. "We
wouldn't mind hearing what happened from you."

"Am I being detained?"

"Not officially, we just—"

"Then no comment."

Traffic continued to stand still and then it was the police officers as well as Vince who found themselves the target of the motorists' insults. The other officer set about attempting to fold up the parachute that had covered half of the road while Vince turned away but found himself again blocked by the policewoman.

"You're not detained just now, but if we suspect you've committed a crime, then maybe you will be," she said, her tone much harsher than that she had used until that point.

"I haven't committed any crime, I've been the subject of an assassination attempt in a helitaxi jacking. I have a flight to catch, and I really don't want you to be the reason I miss it."

"Where's your flight to?"

"I don't have to tell you that."

"Oi! Pig!" someone in a nearby car yelled. "Get out of the fucking road!"

The officer's hand fell to the gun holstered at her side. "Helitaxi emergencies don't happen by accident. Your refusal to cooperate only tells me that you're hiding something. What is it?"

"I'm exercising my right as a citizen of the City of London to refuse to answer questions without detainment. If it's a bribe you're looking for, you're on the wrong side of the border. Crossing isn't far. They're always looking for immigrants. And if you attempt to unlawfully detain me then I won't hesitate to exercise another of my rights."

"You're threatening me?" The other officer had collected most of the fabric blanketing the road and was oblivious to the escalation as they focused on the untangling of the sprawling network of rope.

"I'm stating my intention to defend myself should you yourself breach the law by arbitrarily arresting me. I would like to leave and catch my flight. You can carry out an investigation on your own time. There is no requirement that I comply."

The altercation had lasted long enough that the media had caught wind of it, as indicated by the arrival of several drones from the east. Their cameras bore down upon the bickering pair with ominous curiosity as the policewoman withdrew her hand from her side, the malice in her expression amplified as Vince took measured steps back towards the pavement. When it became clear that she didn't intend to confront him in front of the cameras, he turned around and walked away at a speed indicating urgency but not suspicion. One of the drones followed him, but he just put on his mask and glasses before turning around and disabling the camera with a flourish of his laser pointer.

This time, Vince hailed a normal taxi and morphed into the traffic as the commotion grew busy with the arrival of the mercenaries in their fleet of SUVs. Peering out the back of the saloon's tinted windows, he watched as the police did exactly nothing to intercept them, both parties hounded by the growing flock of drones that hadn't been able to even attempt to give chase to the fleeing hitman. Soon enough, he was deposited at the gates to Heathrow Airport where he retrieved his phone and dialled a number reserved for the rare occasions on which he found himself travelling on a public commercial flight.

"Svitlana," Vince greeted, the phone answered before the first ring had even elapsed.

"Identification code," a harsh Slavic voice barked back.

"VF-090976."

"Passcode."

"160575."

"Please transmit a fresh biometric signature."

Vince navigated through an application within his neural chip and captured an instance of his personal biometric identity, sending it promptly to the contact he had saved for Svitlana Orestivna. She was a fixer who specialised in the smuggling of goods and weapons through the airport, one of the many nodes in the network of contacts that enabled Vince to carry out his work efficiently and in the manner that had garnered him his reputation. After a brief delay in which she verified the information he had given, they arranged a place to meet. He provided her with his gun and had it thrust unceremoniously back into his hands when he touched down in Chicago several hours later.

He picked up the Mazda from the garage near the airport and drove promptly to Omaha, stopping only to refuel when absolutely necessary. The sun was descending below the horizon when he arrived and the police were still very much present at the site where Noah's neural chip had emitted its last signal.

Vince found himself on the receiving ends of several anxious barrels as he rolled up to the scene of the crime and stepped out of the car. He raised his hands in pre-emptive surrender as the police officers descended upon him like moths to a flame.

"Identify yourself!" one of them barked, stepping forwards to break the circle.

"Ain't that the killer?"

"Can't be. He's too thin."

"Where is he?" Vince asked back. "Where's the body?"

"I don't know who the hell you think you are, but this is an ongoing police investigation. Do you have relevant information to the case?"

"He was my friend. I want to know where he is. I want to know what happened to him."

"Who was your friend, honey? The one who got shot or the one who got away?"

"Noah Cox," Vince growled. "Where is the body? And what happened to him?"

"Your friend got involved in an altercation. Wrong place at the wrong time. It looks like a hit, but we're yet to find out why and the person who did it escaped. Do you have anything you want to tell us?"

"No." Vince found himself again drenched in emotion, though this time, it was nothing but anger. Volatile anger which threatened to unleash itself upon the officers that retained their defensive stance, upon the pavement below his feet, and upon the buildings lining the neon-lit streetside. "No, there isn't. But I want information from you. Who did it?"

"I'd give you a name if we had one. But we're yet to get a match. Suspect is not a U.S. citizen. We're having to ask the Europeans for information, and you know what they're like."

"But you've got a face. Camera footage."

"That we do. But like I said, no match on it. Not in the American, Canadian, English, Japanese, or London database. It's just wrangling with the bureaucrats, now. Unless the guy's from around Russia or China, in which case we're not gonna get him so easily."

"Can I see the footage?"

"You're not a journalist, are you? If you think you could help us identify him, then go ahead. You got a chip?"

Vince nodded and enabled the receipt of untrusted communications through his neural chip as the police officer finally relaxed his stance and fiddled with a tablet, his brow furrowing as he swiped through a stream of content on the device before finally settling on something that soon arrived in the form of a notification on Vince's HUD. He accepted the transmission and promptly reenabled his security settings before watching the video that had embedded itself in the corner of his vision.

The view of the busy street was static at first and nothing appeared immediately amiss. That changed very quickly when a car waiting in traffic veered over to crash into another, and it was only after the passengers of both escaped from the immobilised wreckage that Vince understood what was happening. It was also the first time that he saw Noah's killer's face as he emerged from his car and was almost taken out by Noah's faster reactions. He thought that the police were right to assume he would appear in a European database—his features appeared ethnically Slavic and his fashion was coldly eastern, not unlike Vince's own. He was tremendously broad and stocky, overbearingly so, and Vince found it a miracle that he only took one bullet with the sheer space he occupied.

It was at that point that police sirens became audible over the recording as the traffic behind the affair scrambled to escape. Police officers soon arrived to encircle the location in which Vince found himself standing and orders were hollered over loudspeakers as the pair of hitmen sheltered in limbo beside their respective vehicles. The tension was tangible through the recording and he felt his heart beat faster as events unfolded in a way he knew were going to happen, but it was still painful to watch.

The tension snapped and they rose in unison to fire upon each other. To Vince's delight, he watched the stone-faced assassin take a bullet to the shoulder as Noah was knocked backwards by one himself. And then, just as abruptly as events had occurred, the video cut out.

"What happened?" he asked, the sudden return to the darker night-time street taking him momentarily aback. "Why did it cut out?"

"That was all the relevant footage," the officer exclaimed. "He drove off after that and we were left to deal with your friend's body."

Vince raised his gaze to meet the officer's and they stood, eyes locked, for what felt like a very long time. It was the officer who looked away first, glancing over towards the hitman's car. "Those are some nice wheels."

"You're not telling me something," Vince said calmly. "In fact, you're lying to my face. It doesn't take much from the video you've just shown me to discern what really happened."

The officer resumed the stern expression he had borne upon Vince's initial arrival to the scene, only this time, it felt much colder. "You got what you wanted. In fact, you haven't even given us anything back. We're not doing charity here. So tell us—can you tell us who that guy is? Or are you wasting our time?"

"You killed him." Vince continued to ignore everything the officer said as he took measured, careful steps towards him. "He could have survived that shot. What's one round? It didn't even hit his chest, the way I saw it."

"Look, our officers did what they had to do in the heat of the moment—"

"You murdered him. Not the hitman. You."

The police officer cocked his gun and retrained it on Vince's head, stopping him in his tracks. "Our officers eliminated an armed suspect in an unpredictable situation. We had no idea who he was and we had no idea that he was defending himself. There was nothing to tell us who was what. Only two guys with guns, neither of who talked to us at any point to let us know they were innocent."

Vince clenched and then relaxed his fists. "He was at the hotel. He helped you then. There was no lack of communication on his part. That's all on you."

"Our officers did nothing out of line," the officer growled, his resolution unwavering. "But you, whoever you are, coming here and interfering? That's borderline. So I suggest you get back in your stupid old car and drive far from here. I don't know who you think you are, but we're the police, damn it. We're the police in the post-war world. Folks like you might've had it easy twenty years ago, but that's not how it is anymore. And if you're at all linked to that guy in the video—I'm not gonna make any assumptions—then you know that damned well."

He lowered his gun and nodded in the direction of the car. "Make the smart decision. Nothing you can do can change what happened. So how about you do what every other level-headed person does in this modern world and look out for yourself?"

Vince turned and sauntered to his car, taking a deep breath as he turned the key and rolled back into the street, the officers stepping carefully out of his way. He managed to book a last-minute flight back to London from the city's airport, though he had to abandon his gun in the car. That wasn't terribly obstructive, as it was easy enough to buy another after he landed back in Heathrow. His usual pistol wasn't available commercially, but the shopkeeper wasn't hesitant to offer his recommendation when asked for the intended application.

"The targeted killing of one individual in controlled circumstances," Vince said.

The shopkeeper exhaled sharply, his face breaking into a slight smile. "Yeah, alright. Well, I'd say it depends how many shots you want. If you fancy yourself some insurance as to cartridge size, go with a Glock or one of the new Smith and Wessons. Don't touch the Hollands—they still haven't worked out how to make a half-decent consumer-grade weapon in the twenty years since they've started trying. You have much experience? What do you usually shoot?"

"Heckler and Koch, MK 23."

"That's an old model. You never had a problem with it?"

"I did my due maintenance."

"And isn't that a spec ops weapon? You know what, I'm not going to ask any more questions. If you want to stick with Heckler, you can get a new USP in any of three calibres, including your forty-five. And that's consumer-grade, so you won't get side-eyes from any coppers. How about it?"

"How much for that and a pack of hollow points?"

"The gun, you're looking at about seven grand. I'll throw in the bullets for another two hundred."

"Do you have silencers?"

"Uh, yeah. One for that model, I can make it ten grand, all in."

"I'll take it. Do you take crypto?"

Vince found himself overwhelmed by fatigue as he left the gun shop with the new USP in his holster. The last place he intended to rest was his own home, so instead he rented a car under one of his fake identities and booked into a hotel with the worst reviews he could find. The building was crumbling, the amenities were dysfunctional, the bedsheets were yellowing and stained. But the staff accepted cash and the CCTV was as out of order as the air conditioning. He triggered himself to sleep with his neural chip and woke up with hours to spare before the soirée.

CHAPTER 25

"You're gonna need to rest a while. The bullet didn't cause any permanent damage, but the wound isn't a pretty one. And if you don't want chronic shoulder pain, you need to take it easy for probably a month or two."

Aurel winced as the doctor tightened the last of the stitches over the wound where Noah's bullet had been embedded.

"I can't do that," Aurel hissed. "I have a job to finish. Has my car been fixed?"

"I don't know, they're not my mechanic. Take it up with the boss."

Aurel picked up his phone and dialled Maddox's number, the oligarch answering with his usual haste.

"I was about to call you, actually, AK. I hope you're well enough to catch a flight to London. I've been told Vince has been spotted back here after a noisy little excursion to go see his friend you killed. Now I'm not entirely sure what his plan is, but I've got people watching his house and he's not there. You're going to have to do some digging, but I do have an engagement tonight that, if I were Vince Foster, I would not pass up. So perhaps position yourself at Blenheim Palace this evening. Also, your car's been repaired. Leave soon."

Maddox hung up and Aurel hauled himself out of the bed in the unassuming warehouse in which he had ended up. The doctor attempted to protest but Aurel ignored them entirely as he sauntered through the wide empty space, lit only by thin sun shafts filtering in through greying windows beneath the roof on one side of the room. His shoulder ached and any attempt at excessive movement was met with sharp pain, but the fact that it didn't throb with each heartbeat was an immediate improvement.

He pressed open the stiff metal door to leave the warehouse, standing with his back to the corrugated wall as he took in the endlessly long country road flanked by sweeping fields of wheat and soy. With his neural chip he emulated a hit of nicotine while he waited for the mechanic to arrive with his car.

The sound of heavy tyres eventually disrupted the peaceful monotony and a recovery vehicle hosting the repaired Audi arrived out front, spraying up a cloud of dust from the sandy ground. Aurel arranged to fly privately to London in one of Maddox's private jets with space for him and the car. He slept on the plane and the day was drawing towards its end as he landed in Heathrow and sped across the border, eager to make it to the Oxfordshire estate before the event began, and especially eager to make it there before Vince.

The sun was setting as he arrived at the usually fortified gates, though they were wide open to allow the stream of luxury cars hosting London's most powerful to enter. There was a security presence, though woefully inadequate for the scale of the event, Aurel thought. He approached the gate in much the same way as everyone else but was stopped by one of the guards.

"Identification, please," they said.

"I'm security for Oliver Maddox."

"Identification."

Aurel reached into the inside pocket of his coat and retrieved his genuine European identification documents, the guard spending enough time scrutinising them to cause traffic to build up onto the adjoining road.

"You're not on the list," the security guard finally declared, handing back Aurel's documents. "I'm afraid I can't admit you."

"Do you want me to call Maddox so he can tell you himself? I need to get in."

"We'll have a chat with Mr Maddox when he arrives and tell you what he says. Now, please, make some space for the other guests to come in."

Aurel wanted to argue back but decided against it, instead dejectedly reversing and idling in the layby outside

of the gate. The opulent convoy that had assembled behind him began to progress forwards as the Slovak found
himself overcome by an uncharacteristic sense of paranoia. His eyes darted between each of his mirrors, scour-
ing the leafy surroundings for nothing in particular. Cars
passed routinely by and he felt his heart beat faster with
each one in turn. A bus stop across the road sat perpetually
empty, its lonely bench awash with an eery white glow.

Aurel left his car and strode determinedly to the gates,
where his way was promptly blocked by the security personnel not preoccupied by admittance.

"I don't have time to wait for Mr Maddox to arrive. I can
call him right now and he will tell you to let me in."

The crossed rifles barring his path were unyielding.
"Clear off."

"Someone is going to infiltrate this event tonight and try
to kill Oliver Maddox. I am his security. You are putting
him at risk by refusing me entry."

"We've got plenty of security. Do you know something
we don't?"

"I've been hired specifically to protect him from this individual."

"And we've been hired specifically to protect anyone
from any random freaks. Like you. Clear off."

He was thrust forcefully aside and stumbled back towards his car, where he returned to the driver's seat and
rolled contemplatively in the direction of the neighbouring
town.

Woodstock was quiet on a busy day, and in the evening
it was a ghost town. Aurel regretted not scouting the area

beforehand, because he didn't know where to begin with the search for Vince. What he did know, or rather assumed, was that he wouldn't be entering through the front gates.

The original stone wall encircling the estate was flanked by a distasteful barbed wire fence along its entire length, and the remnants of the old entrance to Blenheim Park had long since been locked up. Aurel followed the entire border of the estate around, searching zealously for a weak point but finding only intact fence and rolling cameras. As he passed over the northern boundary of the estate, he found a single-track road leading into an area cloaked by forest but at the end of it was only met with another wooden barrier.

He reversed out at speed and continued to follow the road along, not stopping to pull over before retrieving his phone and ordering it to dial Oliver Maddox. This time, Aurel was the first to speak, with an urgency that rarely revealed itself. "Maddox. Are you at the event?"

There was a slight pause and the humming of background noise before the oligarch provided his response. "Not just yet. Why, has something come up?"

"They refused my access through the front gate until you arrive. I can't find another way through and I don't know what Vince's strategy will be. You need to stay safe."

A prolonged sigh drifted through the phone. "I have to go to this, AK. I can't afford to be unprotected—you need to work something out. I can't pull strings the same way I usually can when I'm surrounded by this lot."

"I don't need you to pull strings, I just need you to get me inside before Vince. I don't—"

"If you can't get inside, then how are you expecting Vince will? I've hired you to kill Vince, so I fucking expect you to be a step ahead of him. Where is he right now?"

Aurel gritted his teeth before issuing his answer. "I don't know."

"Well, aren't you just incredible value for money. Fucking find him! And don't call me again unless you're standing over his cold fucking corpse!"

The line broke off abruptly and Aurel clenched his hand into a fist, grinding his gritted teeth as he stamped on the accelerator and veered to overtake the line of cars occupying the road before him. He didn't slow down as the speed limit fell with the reintroduction of the town and raced precariously through the light evening traffic. He narrowly missed obliterating a pedestrian as they chose the wrong moment to attempt to cross the road. Warnings blared from the car's computer as he then jerked the wheel to correct himself, an oncoming van careening onto the pavement to prevent a head-on collision. In his peripheral vision, Aurel noticed several onlookers speaking hastily into their phones and it spurred him only to drive faster, and he was clear of the boundaries of the town long before the police appeared to stop him.

He reached the northern road he had inspected once before and lurched around the corner, wheels screeching as he held his foot to the floor. There wasn't as much space to build up speed as he would have liked, but the car was still travelling with immense speed as it met the barrier. The gate burst open and his airbags did, too.

The car spun out of control and no attempt at correction could have saved Aurel as he skidded through the showering shards of wood and rammed one of the many trees lining the isolated road head on. The Slovak's head rocked forward and bounced off the airbag, a great shot of pain whipping through his neck as warning signs lit up like fairy lights across the HUD and dashboard.

With a grunt and another bout of pain, Aurel gripped the door handle and thrust himself out of the wreckage of the vehicle. He stood still for a moment, listening intently for any sound but hearing only the rustling of leaves, the twittering of birds, and the hissing of the car as steam drifted from its ruined underside.

Aurel was not deterred. He grabbed a backpack full of necessities from the boot and began to walk. The CCTV camera overlooking the battered entrance didn't go unnoticed; the smaller camera nestled into one of the nearby trees, however, did.

CHAPTER 26

"Hello. Am I speaking to Christie West's head of security?"

Vince sat patiently in his car at the side of the main road, several miles away from the estate where guests were supposed to arrive in exactly two hours' time.

"Yes. Who is this?" The man at the other end of the phone bore an implicit impatience in his tone, indicating to Vince that not a single word could be wasted.

"An unauthorised individual will attempt to intrude upon the event taking place at Blenheim Palace tonight. They will be armed. It is likely they will attempt to pass themselves off as an authorised guest or member of a particular guest's security team. You cannot allow them to enter."

"How do you know this? Who is this?"

"Please give me your assurances that this individual will not be allowed access to the event."

"Nobody without prior authorisation was ever going to be allowed access to the event. Miss West takes security very seriously. Now, please, identify yourself."

Vince put down the phone and started the car.

The renovations made to the estate's security under Christie West's ownership had made access from any-where but the main entrance much more difficult than in the past. In his assessment, Vince had identified three pos-sible weak points—a steel gate at an intersection along the northern border of the grounds, a wooden gate on the same road earmarked for deliveries, and an unassuming mechanical gate nestled along a road some ways away from the actual palace itself.

Vince didn't think the first of these the likely point of intrusion for Maddox's hitman—although the road beyond the gate ran straight to the palace, the gate itself was sturdy and locked. Not the mention artistically intricate, too.

The latter option he also thought unlikely. Not only was it inconspicuous, but it was also directly adjacent to a house completely irrelevant to the palace grounds. It was a low gate, so it could have been vaulted on foot, but then it would have been a mile and a half to walk to get to the ac-tual palace. It was, however, the only entrance of the three not covered by surveillance. Vince changed the fact with the affixing of one of his own cameras to the side of the house.

That's why Vince felt confident about his chances as he rolled to a stop at the side of a bridge overlooking the

River Glyme, where he clambered down to the bank and used an electrical pump to quickly inflate his kayak. It didn't have much in the way of storage space, but he didn't need much. He carried his pistol in his holster, his phone in his pocket, and two more cameras in his coat. It sufficed.

He drifted up the river, fighting against the current but travelling well within the time he had allotted for the endeavour. There was nothing to observe in the way of human activity along the footpaths lining the riverside on his right. It was silent, eerily so. He had expected to at least be able to hear the distant thrum of music, but that hadn't yet begun. Neither, apparently, had the shifts of any security guards, if it was in their remit to patrol the boundaries of the estate.

The stone tips of protrusions from the height of the palace peeked over the dense thicket guarding the embankment. The river widened with Vince's continued journey northwards, an offshoot appearing to the left that the hitman ignored as he continued along his winding route to end up at the base of a great stone bridge connecting the landmasses on either side of the water. A grand arch beneath its centre was split into two small openings, neither of which were quite large enough to allow the passage of a person in a boat. It was here that Vince rowed himself to the shore and let the air out of the kayak, folding it up and stashing it in an adjacent cluster of trees where it wouldn't be so easily spotted.

Vince now had precisely one hour until guests would begin to arrive. He walked at pace down the long road towards the first of the northern gates, covering a mile and a half in twenty minutes. The road was uncomfortably exposed, with great strips of trimmed grass making the area one of the most open in the area. Lines of trees occupied the space beyond, though, so Vince took shelter under these as he made the trek.

The camera watching the entrance only covered the exterior, allowing Vince to invisibly attach one of his cameras to the gate's decorative black steel frame. He then proceeded towards the location of the last of the entrances, cutting through a stretch of trees and tracing the edge of a field to come to a tidy dirt track exiting a small forest. With half an hour left, he followed this along until he could walk no further without being sighted on the cameras fixed to the top of the new fence behind the old stone wall.

He spent no more than thirty seconds casting his eyes across the available trees before choosing one with a suitable view in which to place his last camera. He then briskly recounted his journey up the dirt road and continued on until he found himself back at the bridge where he had stashed the kayak. It was here that the two long roads from the northern gates joined together, and it was here that Vince hoped to intercept Maddox's hitman if he behaved as Vince predicted.

The eventual muted throb of music arose when there were ten minutes to spare before the event's scheduled start time of seven-thirty. Vince sat in the tree cluster with the deflated kayak, eyes flitting systematically from the river to the bridge to the northern roads and then each of the camera feeds in turn. The motion and audio detectors irritatingly triggered on the camera on the steel gate every time a car drove past on the adjoining road. There was also some noise picked up by the camera on the quiet gate on the western side, which Vince ascertained only to be the muffled bickering of whoever lived in the house next to it. For a long while, he sat in quiet anticipation, beginning to feel cold as the cool evening air permeated the thin protection offered by his coat.

Half an hour after the guests were supposed to have begun to arrive, Vince received an unexpected message from Monty.

Mr Foster. Have you arrived?

Vince glanced over the camera feeds before dictating his response. *I've been waiting inside for some time. Maddox has hired another hitman to kill me who I also expect to make an appearance. Do you know if Maddox has arrived?*

I haven't seen him myself. But things are moving slowly with the front gate. There are a lot of identities to check. I will personally be refraining from excessive drink, so, if you happen to find yourself amongst the crowd, I should hopefully remain of use. But I would prefer we were not sighted together.

It goes without saying. Now I have to get back to watching some cameras. Let me know when Maddox arrives.

It was perhaps ten minutes later when the motion sensor on the steel gate produced a hit of actual interest to

Vince. When he went to respond to the notification, there was nothing to see, but when rewinding the footage he caught a glimpse of a black saloon driving past at exceptional speed. Initially, he thought nothing of it, but upon a slowed-down inspection he could make out the faintest trace of the features borne by Maddox's hitman, judging by the imagery he had seen in the footage from the American police.

He did nothing in the way of immediate response. He only continued to wait. The last of the natural light was eliminated with the disappearance of the sun and Vince was left to rely on what little visibility was offered by the moon, the bridge glowing a soft white and his hideaway plunged into darkness.

The music grew louder and lights danced in the distance. Spotlights cut through the air above the palace and the repeated roar of laughter tumbled across the green towards the water. Vince found himself offering cursory glances towards the building between checks on each of the security feeds, noticing the silhouettes of several individuals breaching the confines of the courtyard where the bulk of the festivities were taking place. They wandered, or rather staggered, onto the path that split into three outside of the entrance and carried on straight, in the direction of the bridge, drunkenly cackling and chattering without break. Vince cursed quietly to himself as they painstakingly slowly made their way onto the bridge and paused to look over the river, not in the slightest way aware of the hitman's presence in the trees only metres away.

A notification buzzed on Vince's phone and he flipped over to the feed from the entrance with the wooden gate, only to see that the gate no longer existed. In its place were hundreds of shards of what used to be the gate alongside the same black saloon he had seen in the footage from the camera beforehand. It had crashed into one of the trees by the gate, and climbing disjointedly from its steaming wreckage was the hulking figure of Maddox's hitman, whose name Vince was still yet to discover. He appeared to be unharmed, though a slight grimace contorted his face as he carried out the awkward manoeuvre.

The hitman stumbled to the back of the car and retrieved a bag, his eyes loosely tracing his surroundings and sweeping across—but never fixating on—the camera through which Vince watched his every move.

The path from the gate was almost two miles away and, if Maddox's hitman moved with the same relaxed gait as he did in the time before he left the view of the camera, Vince had at least half an hour until he would make an appearance on the bridge. The inebriated party guests, however, were still present, and showed no intention to leave. His hand fell uncertainly to his holstered pistol, the suppressor on which would have rendered any shots inaudible to the rest of the guests.

He withdrew his hand from his side and stepped carefully towards the path leading left where it forked beyond the bridge, remaining concealed beneath the alders lining the riverside. When he had moved far enough that he couldn't make out the figures of the drunks, he stepped out from beneath the trees and carried on down the path, at a pace that could only tenuously still be described as a walk.

Vince felt terribly exposed as he traversed the park, aiming to reach a fork just over half a mile from the bridge, the last possible location at which Maddox's hitman's path could deviate from Vince's. Like much of the park, the path was lined by swathes of short grass and various deciduous trees placed sparsely throughout. Thicker clusters were barricaded into isolated sections by fences, as was the case when Vince reached the fork, his heart pounding, a fresh sheen of sweat glistening upon his forehead. He had to choose between adequate cover for an ambush and close enough range to take an effective shot. In the end, he decided upon an oak in the patch of greenery at the centre of the intersection, its bough only just wider than he was.

Silence. Vince had travelled far enough that the sounds of the party were only an afterthought in the backdrop of the quiet hum of nature. A soft wind caressed the trees under which he waited, tousling the leaves above his head. Plants that he thought could only have been crops in the neighbouring fields rustled at a volume that was so quiet yet overwhelmed all else. He was aware of his every breath, his chest rising and falling in a controlled manner as he steadied his focus and checked routinely over his shoulder for the approaching figure of the European hitman. Not just along the path, which turned gently to the left and cut off not far beyond his field of view, but against the shadows of the lonely trees and the fences sectioning off further areas of the park. It wasn't that Vince wasn't confident he had the element of surprise, but the fact that if it had been him, he would never have travelled so brazenly along the open road.

Vince knew his opponent was capable and ruthlessly efficient, and he didn't underestimate him at all. But he also, from what Vince had gathered, lacked care. His opponent was arrogant, and the hitman was hedging all his bets on the hopeful estimation that this behaviour would remain consistent. Despite it all, at no point would he let himself succumb to complacency.

A soft series of sounds emerged from beyond the corner around which Vince couldn't see. Footsteps—heavy, from thick-soled boots. Grunting. Deep, rapid breaths. The European hitman moved with urgency, and his eyes devoured the scenery as he pressed into it. But he couldn't see Vince.

It was impossible to tread silently through the grass.

CHAPTER 27

Aurel marched with frustrated purpose, his coat tight against his rapidly rising and falling chest. He rued the loss of his car with each forceful step along the seemingly limitless track, pavement having appeared at some point since emerging from the forest cover.

The pain in his shoulder had returned from a period of subtlety, each movement sending a sharp pang along his entire side. But he was too focused on his constant, encompassing anxiety to care for the discomfort.

For an estate apparently hosting some of the world's most powerful, Aurel thought it to be terribly empty. The forest, as small as it was, was almost quaint. Outside of that, he thought it comparable to barren farmland. Plain, short swathes of grass, neat rows of trees, and fields of some crop he didn't recognise. At least, he thought they were crops.

He walked through an arrangement of silent buildings that probably would have been occupied had he been there during the day. An owl hooted and the Slovak snapped his view to meet its gleaming eyes in the trees that rose along the road leading from the compound. The hair stood up on the back of his neck.

A notification on his phone incited a sharp curse in his mother tongue and he slowed his rapid pace to read it.

I'm here, a message from Maddox read. A second came through immediately afterwards. *Where is Vince? Is he even here?*

Aurel contemplated his options and, after slowing to a complete stop, decided against any response at all. He switched the device off and pocketed it before carrying on along the road towards the palace.

Uncertainty was the enemy of many. Of politicians, of businesspeople, of just about anyone who relied upon a particular level of predictability to go about their routine. The uncertainty that racked Aurel would usually have been enough to deter him from pressing ahead with his duty, had the job been for a less influential employer. With Maddox, the Slovak knew almost for a fact that to leave the oligarch vulnerable was to invite him to hire yet another assassin to hunt him, just as he had been hired to hunt Vince.

There hadn't been a great deal of time between Aurel's killing of Noah Cox and the party he found himself approaching. He would have liked to have been able to prepare more. Cameras, informants, sensors, positionings. He had none of these things. He just had, so he hoped, the element of surprise. Vince didn't know that he would be there—but then, neither did he know for sure that Vince would, either.

A few hundred metres down the road from the compound brought him to the convergence of a fork. The palace was still out of sight, only unimpressive stretches of greenery mostly cloaked in darkness by the night.

Vince's gun didn't make any noise as he raised it. His footsteps did, though that didn't end up mattering.

CHAPTER 28

After unloading a single bullet into the back of the hitman's head, Vince finally learned his name. Digging through his pockets had produced a wallet with an identity card. *Aurel Kostra*. He had never heard of him.

He liberated the corpse of a holstered gun, switching on its safety and lowering it into his coat pocket, and a phone. Turning it on allowed him to view a series of notifications from an angry Maddox.

Well? Are you going to answer?

If there's someone here tonight who's going to kill me, I need you to fucking respond. I don't want to be forced to leave on your behalf.

Fucking useless cretin. GIVE ME A FUCKING UP-DATE!

Vince returned the phone, cautious of the possibility of its location being tracked, and then, in the very same line of thought, picked it back up and began to walk back towards the palace.

More guests had made their way out of the barricaded courtyard, flooding the paved walkway down towards the river and the gardens beyond. When Vince appeared, nobody looked at him twice. He was one face amongst hundreds and his dark attire practically blended him into the moonlit nightscape.

He moved faster and faster through the dispersed clusters of partygoers. The gate that had stood resolutely shut had so easily resigned and now hung open, a pair of guards lazily watching over the free entryway with weapons slung inattentively over their shoulders. Their attention, although it remained upon the guests, seemed to fixate rather on their appearances than the possible threat to their security, judging by the way they gawked at each passer-by. When Vince passed between them and into the courtyard, they didn't bat an eye.

The tranquillity that had existed in the estate's gardens was entirely absent amid the throbbing heart of the gathering. At the centre of several larger crowds were faces Vince recognised as oligarchs—some of which he knew personally from jobs he had done for them in the past. Immediately through the gates there was also a heightened security presence, though not for the event generally, but in the form of teams accompanying each oligarch individually. They did not share the same lax outlook as the personnel hired for the event, and Vince felt suddenly so very exposed as his black attire transformed from camouflage into a beacon amongst the sea of garish colours, drawing the recognition of all those dressed in just the same way.

A phone in his pocket buzzed and he didn't know if it was his or Aurel's. Several pairs of eyes bore into him through tinted glasses as he weaved through the throng, aiming to reach the entrance to the palace itself where he expected to find Oliver Maddox. He had no evidence to suggest this would be the case, only counting on the hope that the oligarch's paranoia would have drawn him away from the open space and into the building and the concealment it provided.

Towards one of the corners of the courtyard Vince spotted Montgomery Sharp, a glass of champagne in one hand and a woman probably fifty years his junior in the other. He wore a suit much smarter than the chequered shirt he had been wearing the last time their paths had crossed and his mouth rocked with raucous laughter. His eyes met Vince's and in that moment the hitman recognised his inebriation was a façade. The oligarch was just as present as he was and made it clear in his masked expression that he needed to tell him something.

Vince finally stopped moving, taking refuge next to a planter on an elevated platform at the courtyard's edge, and retrieved both phones from his coat. He found one notification from Maddox on Aurel's phone.

I can see you moving towards the palace. Are you really ignoring me?

While a much curter message from Monty suddenly lit up Vince's HUD.

Maddox is inside.

The two made eye contact once more and communicated their next move wordlessly.

Vince crouched down and left the phone on the floor before proceeding to stride along the edge of the courtyard, making his way behind the group in with Monty at its centre. His core began to feel uncomfortably warm, his urgency driving out the permeating cold that hung in the night air.

If the security presence in the courtyard was heavy then in the palace's entry hall it was impermeable. Two event guards stood across from each other in the wide doorway and further legions of personnel lined the borders of the much smaller groups that surrounded the most influential guests. Vince slowed his pace so as not to arouse suspicion and forced himself to be subtler in the way he swept his eyes through the crowd. He struggled to isolate any particular individuals through the uniforms and gun barrels, the latter of which felt as if they outnumbered glasses of drink in the spacious hall.

Another message on his HUD prompted Vince to respond immediately.

Can you see him?

Vince pretended to be part of a group of men too drunk to pay him any real heed and sent back a response. *Not yet.*

He stayed mostly stationary for a while, snatching a glass of wine from a passing server and pretending to drink it as he meandered through the room. The music wasn't so

loud inside, a softer mix sifting from speakers nestled behind statues in archways halfway up the walls. Vince found
it much easier to think, to focus. He set eyes upon Christie
West herself, exiting a group of people much taller than
her who had to that point concealed her from Vince's
view. Among them were Alfie Burke, oligarch for Wands-
worth and one of Maddox's closest allies. He, like Maddox
and Monty, owned a sizeable stake in the NHS as well as
controlling the London Underground in its entirety. Vince
spotted John McCarthy, the namesake for the tower in
which he had so recently been apprehended by the FBI,
too. Maddox's allies were plentiful, but Maddox was firmly
absent. He gripped the hilt of the gun in his pocket and
nervously switched off the safety.

Another message came through from Monty as the
guests in the entry hall suddenly began to move towards
the exit. *We've been told Christie is to give a speech. Have
you found him yet?*

He's not here, Vince uneasily replied.

*I saw him go inside ten minutes ago. He can't possibly
have run.*

I'm going to stay back and try to find him.

Vince approached one of the official security guards and
drew their attention with a tap on their shoulder. "Excuse
me. Do you know where I can find the toilet?"

"Just through the door at the back and then at the back
of the room you come into," the guard responded with an
accompanying gesture. "There should be someone stood
outside to direct people. Might be a queue, too."

The guard hadn't been exaggerating about the queue. Vince pressed through the heavy old doors at the end of the lobby and found himself at the back of a disorderly arrangement of what felt like half of the event's guestlist. How many of them were actually waiting for the use of the lavatory, he didn't know. Most of those present appeared, as in the previous room, to be bodyguards.

They were protecting Oliver Maddox.

Vince hadn't realised until the oligarch glanced idly around the room, face alight with a muted fury, which the hitman could only assume derived from the likelihood that he had never had to wait for anything in his life. He wasn't the only oligarch there—Vince took note of one or two more—but he was by far the most protected, surrounded by personnel on all sides.

In a crowd, he didn't look particularly distinctive. He dressed in his typical three-piece suit and bright red tie. His short greying hair was remarkably average. He was the image anyone would have conjured if asked to think of a middle-aged man.

He's here. Vince's breaths transpired with a slight, mostly imperceivable tremble as he pivoted to stand behind a cabinet and waited patiently for a response from Monty. It arrived almost instantaneously.

Do you have a clear shot?

No. I need something to isolate him. He's surrounded.

Would a stampede do?

How do you intend to go about that?

It would only take one shot. These guards are bristling to shoot somebody. Have you seen how bored they are?

Well, do it soon.

Tell me when.

Vince poked his head out from the concealment offered by the cabinet as the queue moved slowly forwards. Maddox had made his way to the front, roughly thrusting away the guide organising the queue and striding through the doorway at the centre of the back wall of the room.

Now.

There was a brief delay in which Vince inched forwards with the rest of the queue, time seeming to stand still and the constant chatter dulling from a racket to a droning hum.

The explosion of the gunshot had exactly the intended effect. The queue fell apart in an instant as screams cut through the air from all directions and every guest responded differently. Some people fell to the floor, some ran in fear. Vince ran, too, though with predetermined purpose.

Maddox's bodyguards were well trained. They stood in a line across the corridor, entirely barricading access to the door through which Maddox waited, even blocking off some of the guests who had been at the front of the queue in doing so. They stood to attention, handguns held cautiously across their bodies—not aimed, but in a position where they very easily could have been.

The panic initiated by the shot began to falter as further shots failed to materialise. The flight of many of the guests meant that the hall behind the lobby was now much emptier, and Vince felt the scrutinous gazes of much of Maddox's security force as they decided what to think of him.

A discordant chorus of heavy footsteps arose from the swarming mass in the doorway. At first, Vince thought they were just bodyguards, but their faces were concealed and they were dressed entirely in black and they weren't armed with pistols, but military-grade assault rifles. And unlike the bodyguards crossing the width of the chamber, they didn't hold these weapons in anticipation of a firefight. They initiated the firefight.

Maddox's security force was caught completely unaware, each of them falling to the ground in sequential turn as the deafening roar of automatic gunfire brought a ringing to Vince's ears. The volley of bullets eviscerated everything in its path, streaks of blood and mangled body parts spattering over the floors and walls of the listed building. It was over in seconds, and to call it a firefight was misleading. A better description would have been an execution.

At some point Vince must have dropped to the floor with the rest of the guests who had chosen not to flee, because that's where he found himself when the momentary gunfire ceased. The mercenaries proceeded to charge over the mix of bodies, alive and dead, a series of intermittent yelps and cries indicating that they weren't taking much care about it.

Vince articulated a message to Monty. *Are these yours?*

There was a slight delay before a response arrived. *Are what mine? I don't know what's going on!*

The mercenaries streamed through the door hosting the bathroom and Vince covered his ears in anticipation of the second round of gunfire. It never happened. The hitman gingerly removed his hands from his ears and pressed himself to his feet, removing his gun from his pocket and holding it in front of him as he carefully traversed through the entangling bodies. He nearly fell victim to the subsequent explosion.

Vince's ears rang again as he flew back with the force of the shockwave. He could hear a pounding through the ringing. His heart. There was screaming, dissonant and echoing.

At his feet laid a dismembered arm. It had flown through the bathroom door and struck him in the midst of the detonation. When he brought a tentative hand to his face, his fingers came away sticky and red.

Something ached. He took a shaky step forward and his head swam and it wasn't an ache anymore. It was a sharp, agonising pang. An alarm was sounding somewhere but Vince couldn't really pinpoint where and people were coughing and crying and a veritable army of bodyguards poured into the crumbling remnants of the bathroom. Some of them stayed behind to escort guests from the room, one of them placing a hand on Vince's shoulder and finding it firmly removed as the hitman's hearing and composure slowly returned to him.

He fought through the throbbing pain and entered the bathroom, having to contort and squeeze through the rubble that had gathered from the collapse of much of the ceiling. The mercenaries that had entered before were in pieces. So was everything else. Water poured from the remnants of the toilet and the sink, which now existed only as scattered shards of ceramic. A window at the centre of the back wall of the room had been deprived of all its glass, only wickedly dangerous jagged edges around its inner borders remaining.

As Vince took note of the shattered window, he felt a sudden pang in his stomach and cast a frantic look over the mutilated bodies and parts thereof, searching each face—the mercenaries' masks had been mostly destroyed by the explosion—and not recognising any of them. Some were mutilated beyond recognition, but the bodies to which they corresponded still did not match the person for which he was looking.

Adrenaline cleared the hitman's head of the daze that had lingered in the wake of the explosion and he practically threw himself out of the window.

A helicopter thrummed on the sprawling field at the back end of the palace. Vince tore through the Doric columns built into the side of the structure with little grace, bounding with exerted strides across the raised platform and almost flying down the steps. He raised his pistol and aimed it at the helicopter, finger hovering anxiously over the trigger. His eyes traced the bodyguards that had escorted the oligarch out of the building, of which plenty remained on the ground. They saw Vince just as Vince saw them, and they readied their own weapons in much the same way he did. There was a moment in which they traded expressions, trying to decode each other, before the hitman finally gave in and lowered his gun.

Maddox's helicopter disappeared into the night sky, travelling firmly in the direction of London as police sirens sounded in the distance. The music had ceased and Vince was soon joined by plenty of others outside the back of the palace. There was no distinguishing factor linking them all—there were bodyguards and members of the palace's security team as well as run-of-the-mill snoops. There were chattering oligarchs who shared expressions ranging from grim to silently pleased. Those in the latter group were few and far between, as the majority of the oligarchs took the opportunity to depart during the chaos.

Vince joined them in doing so himself. He walked westwards, along one of the footpaths crisscrossing the estate. Nobody followed him and he continued until he reached an old bridge across the narrowest part of the river. From there he fought through a dense stretch of foliage beneath a canopy of oak trees and reached a quiet country lane which he followed along until the larger, older stone bridge from which he had set off in the kayak rose to cross the river again before him. His car remained as he had left it.

He swiftly lowered himself into the driver's seat and headed off towards London without looking back.

CHAPTER 29

Vince needed information. To acquire it, he resorted again to Montgomery Sharp, who had sent him a breakdown of the conclusions that had been made following the attack.

They were smuggled in, the message read. *PAL fighters. Nobody's been indicted yet, but everyone's pointing fingers at Maddie Osborne's daughter. Her connections aren't exactly a secret.*

PAL stood for the People's Army of London, a generally far-left guerrilla group established sometime in the aftermath of the city's independence referendum. Most people referred to them as communists, but that was too specific. They were a haven of refuge for the city's Marxists, anarchists, and plain old socialists, provided they exhibited the necessary violent tendencies. The essential criterion to join was an active hatred for the ruling oligarchy and a willingness to fight tooth and nail to remove it, at any cost.

Maddie Osborne was the oligarch for Newham and had been since independence. She wasn't herself a radical, but her daughter, Isobel, had garnered a reputation for being the mouthpiece of the guerrillas in the sphere of the elite. Mouthpiece, prime financier, and now means by which to commit acts of terror. Allegedly.

Vince found it incredible that she had managed to survive to twenty-four, which could probably have been attributed to her residence in the UR. He found it even more incredible that it had been so easy to acquire her contact information. Monty had been hesitantly willing to provide Maddie Osborne's phone number and a further conversation with her had landed him Isobel's. Not two days after the soirée, he found himself waiting alone at a café inside the London City Airport, a location chosen by Isobel after she had agreed to meet him for a matter Vince had only described as, "Politics."

He had nearly finished his first cup of coffee by the time a blonde-haired woman matching Isobel's description entered the café and scoured the busy tables for Vince. She locked eyes with him and he snickered, the corners of his mouth curling into a slight smile as she ambled over to the corner in which he had settled and lowered herself into the chair opposite.

"You're not fooling anyone," Vince said first, eyes cast inattentively towards the door. "But it's the most convincing attempt I've personally seen."

Isobel raised an eyebrow and leaned back in her chair, crossing her arms. "I'm sorry?"

"Okay, maybe if I squint, it almost looks real. Otherwise, nope, I'm afraid you'll need to go back to the drawing board."

The highborn woman cursed under her breath. "Well, fine, but I'm sure you can understand why I take such measures."

"To extend a branch of trust to people when you meet them for the first time is evidently not it."

"Obviously not. I can't trust anyone. Which I'm sure you get. There are a lot of powerful people who want me dead."

"I'm well aware. That's why I've come to talk to you. Or rather this mechanical representation of you, apparently. I need to talk to someone involved in a particular leftist militant group."

The Isobel-shaped android exhaled sharply and smiled. "What was it, then? What gave it away?"

"Your eyes don't move until you've finished swivelling your neck," Vince stated. "It's a very immediate transition from one movement to the other. Too smooth. I was impressed by the gait, though. Most attempts at a lifelike model really struggle to make the gait look natural, but this—whatever this is—was rather fluid. If I was looking the other way, I probably wouldn't have thought anything."

"Well, that's some solace. I have put an immense amount of money into this, so I'm really quite upset that you were able to so easily see through it."

"You put an immense amount of money into something else, as I understand it."

"Oh, yes, of course, that's why you're here. Well, Vince Foster, you know I can't divulge any information without an adequate background check. First question—what do you want with the People's Army?"

Vince tapped his fingers on the table and looked around uneasily. "Do we have to do this here?"

"Half the people around you won't speak a lick of English and the other half won't care. Please answer the question."

"Fine," the hitman sighed. "I want to... hm... *depose* Oliver Maddox."

"Interesting." The android crossed its legs and reclined further. "And why is that?"

"He hired me, betrayed me, and then hired an assassin to kill me and a colleague, who was also my best friend. Is that a valid motivation?"

"Probably more valid than that of half the fighters in the People's Army. So you're something of a fugitive right now?"

"I killed the assassin he sent after me but he's bound to send another. And I'd rather take him out sooner than later if it means I don't have to look over my shoulder all the bloody time."

"I think you'd be destined to look over your shoulder until the day you die if you were to kill Oliver Maddox," Isobel remarked.

"The guerrillas can take the credit publicly," Vince said drily. "I'm not interested in that. This is personal."

"They'll be glad for it. Well, you've stated your intentions—what do you actually want from them in whatever grand scheme you have playing out in your head?"

"I need firepower," Vince declared. "I need fighters. I need a force that will overwhelm the army he has working at his beck and call. Maddox explained to me personally the merits of his security force, and it's not something I would be able to overcome on my own. And on this occasion, I thought the enemy of my enemy could be my friend."

"There's more to this fight than killing one oligarch," Isobel said with a hint of disapproval.

"It's a start. You must agree, otherwise why would you have smuggled in those commandos?"

"I'm not going to comment on that," Isobel said curtly. "What I can tell you is that I believe you are genuine."

The android leaned forwards and revealed a slip of paper which it proceeded to slide across the table.

"That is an address and a code. You go to the address given there at a specific time—I will text you—and ask for Ava Mao. You will be told that she doesn't live there. You then go and say what's on that card. Understood?"

Vince took the paper and deposited it in the inner pocket of his coat without looking at it. "Sounds easy enough. Thanks."

"Be careful, Vince," Isobel added as the hitman rose to leave. "I know it's common sense, but look out for yourself. The oligarchs reside at the centre of the most entangling web of informants and security. Oliver Maddox more so than anyone else. You're playing a dangerous game targeting him on your own."

"I'm not targeting him on my own," Vince said. "I've got help now."

CHAPTER 30

The dank, smog-cloaked alleys of inner London were exactly what Vince had expected of a guerrilla hideout. Although it was early in the morning, the only light came from flickering neon signs barely visible through the encompassing grey haze. Sombre grey office buildings loomed on both sides of the narrow street and rickety connectors zigzagged overhead. Most people Vince passed wore masks, as did he. The same went for possession of a firearm, some of them in poorly attempted concealment. Inquisitive gazes fell persistently upon the hitman as he strode to his destination, the violent undertones of which were not at all well disguised. But Vince ignored them.

The door at which Vince finally arrived didn't stand out from the other homogenous blocks of flats sprawling across the local area. His neural chip told him that the time was two minutes before six, and he waited out those remaining minutes patiently before tapping gently upon the door and stepping back.

"Who is it?" an almost indiscernible voice shouted, muffled, from within.

Vince wasn't keen to shout back, so he only raised his voice slightly when he said, "I'm looking for Ava Mao."

There was a pause and then the twisting of a lock before the door swung open to produce a man of monstrous proportions. His pectoral muscles bulged through his shirt and his jeans could barely contain his legs. He stood much taller than Vince, probably by a margin of about twenty centimetres. The hitman was unfazed, though he did feel suddenly so very small.

"I didn't catch that," the man said bluntly.

"Ava Mao," Vince repeated. "I'm looking for her."

"She doesn't live here."

"I know. She moved to Paris last week."

"You wanna come in?"

"Please."

The man had to turn around and walk away first for Vince to be able to fit through the doorway himself, ensuring he brushed his feet on the dirty mat beneath him. He was gestured through to a living room lit only by faux candles, the lock on the front door clicking behind him as he was then followed up by the hulking man and urged to take a seat.

Her gun clicked with her arrival to the scene. She, like Vince, wore a mask concealing her face, which could just have been due to the pollution. Her anthracite hair sat in a bun atop her head and her red leather jacket glowed more orange in the flickering candlelight. A golden pendant around her neck bearing a Chinese dragon shimmered, too.

"Jewellery isn't very communist," Vince remarked as he stared down the barrel of her pistol.

"Oh, because communists have to be poor and devoid of all personal belongings," the woman snapped. "Me having this necklace just makes me a champagne socialist, doesn't it? I don't really believe in the ideology if I own just one piece of jewellery?"

"I won't mansplain Marx to you, but pretty much, yes."

"Well, good thing the world isn't as black and white as a literal interpretation would have it. And I'll have you know that personal property has never been disallowed under any communist government in history. It's ownership of the means of production. Productive property. Not necklaces."

"You're Ava Mao, then?"

"Yeah, I am. And you're Vince Foster."

"Lovely to meet you, Ava," Vince said with a tinge of sarcasm. "Care to explain this?"

He nodded at the gun and Ava readjusted her grip. "Precaution. You don't think I didn't do my research before you arrived? Isobel was able to find plenty of information about you. Like the fact that you've worked for Oliver Maddox. And that you've more recently been fraternising with Montgomery Sharp."

"You're aware of what I do for a living?" Vince queried.

"You're a gun for hire."

"That's a crude way of putting it. Well, oligarchs are some of my best customers. So therefore I end up working for them."

Ava narrowed her eyes. "Can you see why I might take issue with that?"

"Of course. And I'm sure you're worried about whether my loyalty lies first with the money they offer or my personal goals. Let me reassure you, Ava—retribution against Oliver Maddox is the only thing I want in this world. And I will stop at nothing to achieve it, regardless of whether you help me. It has meant getting help from Monty Sharp, who may be an oligarch but despises Maddox probably just as much as you do. It has meant putting my life at risk as Maddox devotes all his resources to hunting me down and exterminating me. And it has meant seeking out communist guerrillas who probably view the likes of me as bourgeois scum. But I came here with a tenuous hope that we would be able to put aside any predispositions and work together towards a common interest—destroying Oliver Maddox and everything he stands for. Will you work with me on that?"

The only reaction Ava offered was a raising of an eyebrow and a slight smirk. "Was that rehearsed?"

"Not in the slightest," Vince stated.

The guerrilla's gun finally fell and she gestured for him to stand. He did, brushing down his coat and looking at her expectantly as if for further direction.

"What are you looking at me for?" she questioned, as if reading his mind. "You've come to us for help. That implies you have a plan."

"I do have a plan. But it's dangerous. It would be untoward of me to come in here and expect you to put your fighters at risk at my behest. That, and I'd like to present it to the rest of the leadership if you'll agree to working with me."

"I hope you understand that I'll never trust you. I'm willing to work with you. After that, we're done. We know everything we do is dangerous, so that's not a factor that'll put us off a potential fight. What will put us off is a lack of certainty. But I'm not getting that from you." Ava nodded towards the hallway still occupied by the hulking man. "Since it's Oliver Maddox we're going after, it'll be the Camden cell fighting alongside us. This house isn't a base—there's nothing of interest here. I'll take you to meet Commander Amini in Camden Market. We have a control centre in one of the warehouses there and he's in charge of it. You'll need a better disguise than that, though. Place is full of rats."

"What's wrong with this?"

"You dress like a hitman, Vince. It doesn't matter that you can't identify your face, their tech doesn't rely on just that."

"Alright, well, what did you have in mind?"

Ava holstered her pistol and stepped forwards, grabbing Vince's wrist, an action to which the hitman reacted with an instinctive flinch. She noticed this and repeated the motion with tempered fervour, leading him through the corridor and out into the alleyway where she opened her phone and promptly called someone. She spoke in Chinese after picking up, which Vince began to understand in English after the translation plugin installed into his neural chip kicked in.

"...a lift. I'm at the fake house. With the hitman. You don't like the sound of him? Tough. I believe he's legit. And I make the decisions around here, not you. If he acts up, we'll kill him. That's easy enough. Oliver Maddox wants to already. Kind of why I believe him when he says he wants to kill Maddox first... Oh, I don't care. Will you hurry up?"

They carried on through the labyrinthian alleyways, Vince trusting the guerrilla leader blindly as the pair passed mountains of refuse, unconscious beggars, and aggressive drug addicts. Constituents of the latter group had to be fended off on several occasions, though this was a task to which they both took with natural efficiency.

The haze began to let up as weak sunlight filtered through the slight gaps in the rickety buildings towards the boundaries of the slum. A car idled at the side of the road where the alley grew wide enough to allow vehicular traffic and Ava slid into the back seat, encouraging Vince to do the same.

"This is my sister, Lia. Lia, Vince Foster."

The woman occupying the driver's seat bore remarkable physical similarity to Ava—so similar, that Vince quickly discerned the pair to be twins. He reached forwards with the expectation of a handshake but was shunned, Lia staring straight ahead with scorn evident across her countenance.

"Don't be a bitch," Ava snapped, reverting to Chinese, as the car shifted into drive and rolled out into the road. "He has connections that we can exploit."

"You know he can understand everything we're saying?" Lia drawled without looking back.

Ava shot Vince an accusatory glare to which he responded only by nodding nonchalantly.

"Your chip can translate Chinese?"

"It takes a bit to get working, but yes," he said. "It's not perfect but it's got a lot better in recent years."

"Why didn't you think to tell me?"

"I didn't think it was relevant. I thought you would know. This stuff has been around for a good while."

"It has, in his defence," Lia chimed in. "Though not to say I want to defend him."

"How can you possibly feel safe with one of those plugged in all the time?" Ava ridiculed. "You know several oligarchs have stakes in the companies that manufacture and design them. And the semiconductors come from China. Radio interference, electromagnetism, et cetera... you're asking to be turned into a remote-controlled slave. Please tell me that it's at least not a London company that made it."

"There's nothing to worry about. They have legislative approval around the world. I'm sure you can remember as well as I can the hurdles that took."

"Approval around the world? Half of Europe has blanket banned them at a state level. China doesn't allow chips with any foreign element to them. Same goes for Japan, Australia, New Zealand, even the American-installed Russian government did the same. Maybe it is irrational scepticism. But don't you think it's even a little bit justified?"

Vince stifled the urge to outright reject Ava's notion and instead just shrugged. "Maybe. But I tend to trust technology more than people."

"That'd be a solid policy, if not for the little detail that people design technology."

They arrived some time later at an enclave of pre-war flat blocks not far from Canary Wharf, though their demolition appeared to be ongoing, judging by the presence of several fleets of heavy machinery. Lia pulled into a passage running between opposing rows of dilapidated storage containers, stopping and proceeding to idle where the road turned into a dead end.

"Come on. Get out," Ava ordered.

Vince exited the car and looked around cautiously, though the area, entirely surrounded by residential buildings, was eerily devoid of activity. Ava retrieved a set of keys from a bag in the front seat of the car and spent a while looking through them before eventually coming upon one which she inserted into the lock on one of the containers at the end of the row. Lifting the decaying door revealed a collection of all manner of items of clothing in black and various shades of red, and it could very well have been Ava's personal wardrobe. It wasn't just clothes—there were lidded crates neatly lining the perimeter of the container, one of which rested open to present an array of improvised explosive devices. There looked to be enough to take down the foundations of a skyscraper and that was only one crate—Vince didn't open up any of the others to discover their contents.

"Take your pick," Ava said. "This is one of the conditions to working with us. You're looking the part."

"Is that a particularly sound strategy? To advertise your affiliation with a guerrilla faction through your fashion?"

"There's no law against wearing red. Don't be ridiculous."

Vince ran his fingers over a series of coats made of suede and leather and velvet, many of which he found still hosted the tags of the shops from which they originated. Of the youthful jackets he tried, he found all to be hideously garish and was swift to dismiss each of them in turn. He found one item to be satisfactory—a double-breasted wool peacoat in a shade so dark it appeared as more of a purple in the dim light. It wasn't black, but it fit, and it brought the semblance of a pleased smile to Ava's unyieldingly stern visage.

"Are there many more PAL outlets like that?" Vince quipped as they returned to the car.

"Yeah, lots. Decentralisation is key. Both to our policy demands and our strategy. Except most of them don't have clothes. They're for weapons."

Their next stop was Camden Market, pulling over beneath a great rail bridge where the road closed off to vehicles. The cosy cobbled streets throbbed with activity despite a lightly falling rain, every facet of the city's burgeoning population present in the lively marketplace—buying, selling, perusing, pickpocketing, racketing, surveilling.

There was a tangible police presence, though it was the hopelessly conspicuous informants traipsing aimlessly throughout the meandering streets that held Vince's vigilance. They stopped frequently to lean against walls within earshot of groups the hitman would also have deemed visibly suspicious, and several times cast inquisitive glances over Vince and Ava as they rushed past the makeshift stalls occupying the centre of the road and the pushy salespeople within.

Towards the end of the road, they came upon a brick warehouse forming part of the continuous structure defining the marketplace's boundaries. Next to the wider steel door, at that moment closed, was a smaller entryway, the key for which Ava then spent some time finding. It was an older lock, with most of the nearby buildings sporting biometric security measures, Vince observed.

The guerrilla leader found what she was looking for and then cast one last cursory glance around the immediate surroundings before twisting the key and ushering Vince into the warehouse.

Bright light cast the entire open space in white. The room comprising much of the area inside the building was sectioned into several informal compartments—loaded weapon racks lined the walls in one corner of the room while rows of desks hosting glowing computer screens stood adjacent. The weapons were accompanied by other various items of equipment—body armour, bomb components, hand radios, ammunition containers, medical supplies, and plain clothes in colours like those sported in the container where Ava had taken Vince beforehand.

Much of the room comprised a dining area, the same tables that at one end of the room hosted computers instead hosting the voracious fighters of the People's Army and whatever mess remained from those who had neglected to tidy up. Vince searched for the source of the food and found it to be coming from a doorway at the back wall, behind which he assumed to be either a kitchen or an industrial chiller.

What was most overwhelming was the sheer volume of red. Every single person wore it in one way or another, whether it was the primary colour of their outfit or present in the form of little adornments. Badges bore socialist stars and roses and even hammers and sickles, or in the case of those dressed smartly—Vince counted three people wearing suits—it was just the choice of a red tie that signified their allegiance.

Standing at the midpoint of a catwalk halfway up the wall at the back end of the room was a man draped in a flattering cherry biker jacket not unsimilar in style to that worn by Ava, though hers was much brighter. He seemed to take note of the guerrilla leader's arrival and turned into a room behind him, large windows at either side of the door providing a view over the chamber below but situated at such an angle that Vince couldn't see into them from the floor.

They took the steps up to the catwalk and Ava led the way into the room, which Vince could now see housed a round meeting table cluttered with tablets and phones and stray weapons and propaganda posters. A ring of permanent computers lined the walls and a hefty server rack standing to nearly the height of the room occupied one of the corners.

"Introducing Commander Amini of the Camden Corps," Ava announced, looking at Vince and gesturing to the man in the biker jacket. Vince's current perception of the requirements to be in a position of authority in PAL was a permanent severe expression and this new commander conformed to the letter. His eyes were cold, his brows thick and low set. He wasn't frowning, but he was further from a smile.

He wasn't the only person in the room. Several others stood up upon Ava and Vince's entrance and came over to meet them. The hitman shook hands with captains Vera, Crowder, and Lehman as well as officers Soliman and Kader. There was a general sense of apprehension that he found present in all of their demeanours, though none quite matched the outright hostility he had faced from Ava's sister.

"Okay, Vince," Ava said. "This is it. This is us. What's your plan?"

"How familiar are you all with Oliver Maddox?" Vince began. "Really familiar—not just your ideological preconceptions. How many of you have actually spoken to the man?"

He looked around the room for a response and, as expected, received none.

"There are several traits that define him," Vince continued, pacing slowly back and forth. "The most prevalent of which would be arrogance. He thinks he's the centre of the universe—and with the power and wealth he wields, he may as well be, as far as London is concerned. And yet, at no point does this arrogance lead to complacency. If anything, he's paranoid—aggressively so. His security outfit is... vast. Personal security guards prevent anyone from getting close to him. Private investigators and hitmen take out anyone he deems a threat in the field. He has allies across the oligarchy who are willing to prop him up in the event of an attempt on his life or just his grip on power. He owns much of the city's infrastructure and has proven his ability to hijack systems remotely. He managed to escape your ambush at Blenheim Palace and that was the most exposed I've ever seen him. No, Oliver Maddox won't be exposing himself any time soon. We're going to have to force him into the open."

Commander Amini crossed his arms dubiously. "We've tried. We've tried threats, blackmail, letter bombs, the lot. Lo and behold, it's his lackeys that end up taking the hit for him. That, or he minimises the reputational damage through his connections. We worked with some journalists from the Observer to try to incriminate him in a story a few years ago. Testimony from people who'd worked under him, declassified information as to his shady business dealings, intimate details about his personal life. The very same day it was published just so happened to coincide with the European Parliament bombing. Guess who's suddenly not the centre of attention? Whole story evaporates into thin air. They tried to rerun it after everything started to die down and then the journalists named on it were murdered in broad daylight. We live in a fucking criminal state."

"He's powerful, yes," Vince agreed. "But nobody is infallible. If he won't reveal himself, we must strike him where he hides. At the top of his tower."

"Been and tried. We've sent drones and people in helicopters. The windows are impenetrable, even with the likes of rocket launchers. You're not getting through them with anything short of a tank shell."

"I thought about that. And at first I thought we could try something drastic, like a plane. It worked for al-Qaeda in 2001, it would work for us. But I didn't think that would go down very well with you."

"You're not kidding," Ava snapped. "That would very quickly unite all the oligarchs with a mission to destroy us. As of the present, they barely tolerate us. They'll disrupt us if the opportunity arises, but otherwise they don't want to bear the expense of actually going to war with us. No, it needs to be more targeted than that."

"I thought that would be the case. So I thought of the few possible ways to get us into a position where we could confront Maddox personally," Vince said, gesturing agreement with the guerrilla leader. "I have connections to another oligarch—a rival of Maddox's—with people on the inside. They can manufacture a distraction for the building's security and put the place into lockdown. Maddox told me himself that the building's lockdown state involves the disabling of the lifts, so he'll have to take the stairs. Obviously, the closest escape route would be up, so this would be the first thing I need from you. You need to cut off his access to the roof."

"And how do you propose we do that?"

"Occupy it. You said you've tried helicopters before, so try again. If there's even the threat that you might push down into the building, he'll be forced to go down towards the ground floor—especially if you leave the ground free for escape. If everything goes according to plan, he'd sooner make the decision to escape via the ground floor than wait for his security to clear the helipad at the top of the building, and then it's as simple as intercepting him on his way down. No collateral damage."

Commander Amini raised his eyebrows in his first show of approval since Vince had entered the room. "It seems very straightforward."

"Too straightforward." Ava narrowed her eyes. "And it involves another oligarch. We don't work with oligarchs. We kill them."

"You're not working with him, you're exploiting him for your own gain. This isn't a 'the enemy of my enemy is my friend' situation. He can still be your enemy, and I'm sure he probably wouldn't want to be seen in any other way. But he's my ally, and I can use that to achieve our goals."

Some of the captains and officers listening bore poorly shrouded expressions of disgust while others seemed to reflect what Vince could only interpret as quiet admiration.

Ava fell openly on the side of disgust. "Do you view all your allies as tools to get what you want?"

"No. I go to my allies for help when I know they can help me with something that I couldn't do alone. When there's something mutual to be gained. As there is now." The hitman looked steadfastly into the eyes of the guerrilla leader. "This will work. And it will instigate a state of instability that you will be able to further exploit. Let me go make a call and we can do this."

Ava furrowed her brow before nodding. "Alright. The plan has merit, I'll admit. So let's do it. Go."

CHAPTER 31

Montgomery Sharp travelled to the Sharpspace headquarters every morning by helicopter, landing on the roof and taking one flight of stairs down to his office on the top floor. The first Monday back after the soirée, he didn't even make it out of the helicopter.

The first shot eliminated his pilot while simultaneously shattering the cockpit window. The oligarch fell to the ground with his hands over his head as a second shot resonated from nearby and tore through the torso of one of his bodyguards as the rest streamed out of the vehicle and onto the roof. A subsequent eruption of gunfire in the much nearer vicinity indicated to Monty that his security had failed. The fighting continued for several prolonged seconds before the last shot was fired, a hollow echo ringing out across the open sky.

Monty's hands shook as he removed them from the top of his head and he waited expectantly for one final shot. It never arrived, and he stood up, lips pressed anxiously together as he swept his gaze across the band of masked mercenaries surrounding the helicopter. His hands rose to his sides without thought and he took resigned steps onto the helipad, regaining his confidence and his composure with each measured movement.

"Is this it, then?" he asked as the nearest mercenary firmly gripped his arm with a gloved hand. "Maddox has had enough of me?"

"Mr Maddox has some questions for you," the mercenary replied gruffly as another helicopter descended from behind a nearby skyscraper towards the roof of the Sharp-space offices. "Get in."

"He's getting really rather bold, these days, isn't he?" Monty sighed, stepping onto the hovering aircraft. "Where are we going?"

"You'll find out."

The door slammed shut and another mercenary took the seat to his right, holding a handgun readily across their lap.

Monty attempted to notify his head of security of his abduction but each attempt at a message through his neural chip was met with an error. The oligarch sighed and reclined in his seat, staring dejectedly out over the cityscape.

They landed a few minutes later at base of the magnificent offices of the Camden Space Corporation, the building's myriad windows reflecting brilliantly in the direct sunlight with the shine of a fresh wash. Monty was hauled impatiently out of the helicopter and paraded through the entrance, the inquisitive gazes of every occupant of the lobby upon him. He held his head high, acutely aware of the fact that some of his spies must have been present, unless there was more to the operation than Maddox let on.

He entered the lift with three of the mercenaries, one of which brusquely uttered, "Seventy". The doors slid shut and they began to travel upwards at great speed, each floor passing by as a momentary flash of light.

Maddox was waiting for him as they reached the top. The doors slid open and Monty opened his mouth to speak but found Maddox's hands grabbing his shirt and wrestling him into his expansive office.

"You've fucked up, old man," the oligarch seethed, thrusting Monty to the floor. His eyes were bloodshot, his pupils were dilated, and a toxic stench of alcohol wafted from his mouth with every heavy breath. "You've been conspiring to kill me."

"What are you talking about?" Monty growled, attempting feebly to remove the younger, stronger oligarch from atop him. "Get off me, you great ape. Have some bloody class."

"Don't bullshit me, you fucker. Christie gave me security footage from the party. And the dead fucking body of one of my agents was found in the gardens. Killed. Murdered. By someone you know, Monty. Because you met

with him, didn't you, Monty? And he was at the party because you told him to be there, wasn't he, Monty?"

Maddox stood up, releasing the older man before
swiftly aiming a kick at his ribs. Sharp pain exploded
across his side, and then again as Maddox repeated the
motion.

"Everyone else is pointing fingers at Maddie Osborne,
but I think you brought those guerrillas in, didn't you?
Stooping so low as to working with communist terrorists?
What the fuck is wrong with you?"

Monty propped himself up with his elbows and let out a
series of strained coughs. "Get a hold of yourself, you de-
generate. I did nothing of the sort. I had no idea they
would be there!"

"Fuck you, you lying bastard. I would kill you with my
own two hands right now if I didn't need you," Maddox
snarled. "Stand up."

"Whatever you want, I'm not just handing it over,"
Monty enunciated, standing up out of pride rather than
submission. "Not when you're behaving like an imperti-
nent child."

"Oh, you'll give me whatever I want. Because otherwise
I'll destroy you and make you watch. Shall we have a look
at where your husband is right now?"

Maddox took a few steps back and issued a voice command, resulting in the ceiling beyond his desk opening up
and an enormous screen descending from the gap.

"Okay, computer, bring me the feed for Remy Sharp."

The screen lit up with a high-definition livestream focused upon a single man. He was sitting on a bench in

what appeared to be a park, great swathes of greenery and towering oaks occupying the area around him. Children and dogs crisscrossed the fields all around him, birds fluttered periodically between the trees, families and groups of friends bantered joyously on blankets with picnic baskets. Several clashing melodies filled the air with dull noise interspersed by barking and crying and laughing.

"He's out for his morning walk, how lovely," Maddox remarked, clasping his hands together. "Or sit-down, apparently. Do his legs not work?"

Monty's expression was as firm as stone as Maddox cast an evilly expectant grin at him.

"I wonder if he knows he looks like a paedophile when he goes and sits around all those kids. Look at those mums sat next to him. Disgusted. I would be, too, if I was one of them. Dirty fucking man."

Monty sighed. "You've made your point, Maddox, as crude as it is. But I'm not working with PAL, so I'm not going to be able to tell you about them."

"Oh, but you can tell me about someone else," Maddox said aggressively. "You can tell me about Vince Foster. I'm sure you have plenty to say about him. You could start by telling me what you talked about the first time he went to visit you at Sharpspace. What arose from that. You could tell me how he knew to attack the party and knew where to find me. Because he couldn't just find that out on his own, could he? He must have had help, right?"

"Oh, get over yourself, you paranoid sod. Vince Foster came to me because I had a job for him. Nothing to do with you."

A sarcastic smile creased Maddox's face and he rolled his eyes, shaking his head. "You're a fucking awful liar. Try again."

"You know how the whole hitman thing works. I can't give you any details. And if you know Vince Foster, I'm sure you know he's very dangerous. Frankly, I'm more scared of him than I am of you."

"You shouldn't be, because I don't take well to fucking liars. I guess you two didn't communicate about how he was able to get your contact. That's right, Monty, I'm well aware of the fact that he came to you. It was definitely not the other way around. So don't give me this crap about hiring him. Tell me the truth or else your husband"—he gestured to the screen—"gets his walk cut short."

"You know my own forces will have mobilised by now? You've got... maybe minutes before they arrive to demand my release. And you know the consequences if you don't let me go."

"Really?" Maddox chuckled. "I've got a terrible bit of news for you, then. The usual consequences aren't going to apply. You let your forces roll up and I will fucking obliterate them. I won't let a single one of them survive. We've already purged the lot that were guarding Sharp-space and your security is next. If you wanted to roll them up to my front door to make things easier, well, that would be much appreciated."

In his stomach Monty felt suddenly very hollow. "What are you saying, exactly?"

"I'm saying that I've had enough of all this 'power-sharing' and whatnot. It's really gone on long enough and it's just so much wrangling and bickering and bureaucracy and—really, things would be so much smoother with a single leader. I'm sorry, Monty—that's a lie, no I'm not—but you're done. You and your pathetic little enterprise. And your little buddies whose names I can never remember. Do you have a single ally in inner London or is it just the shitholes?"

"If you're being serious, you're playing a very dangerous game. I can't imagine anyone will support you in this endeavour because it will frankly destabilise the city in its entirety. Not a single one of the oligarchs will be enthusiastic about such a move. Nor will anybody in the international community."

"Fuck the international community! We aren't some impoverished African wasteland state, we're the Free City of London, damn it! If I want this to happen, I can make it happen and I can make people like it! The only people I have to impress are enough of the other oligarchs to back me and I think you'll find I've already done that!"

Maddox's breathing was heavy in his feverish anger. He strode animatedly to his desk and poured a shot of whisky, immediately downing it and letting out a strained cough. Then he turned back to the screen and bellowed, "Agent whatever-the-fuck, can you hear me?"

"Loud and clear, sir," a measured, polite voice responded. "What can I do for you?"

"Go over to Remy there and blow his fucking brains out. Make sure you get the look in his eyes on camera."

"As you wish."

The field of view rose higher as Maddox's agent stood up but quickly stabilised as he walked across the stretch of greenery separating the bench on which they had been sitting and the bench across the way, still hosting the oblivious figure of Remy Sharp.

"Don't do it, Maddox," Monty mouthed. "You will achieve nothing."

"Tell me about Vince Foster, Monty!" Maddox shouted at the top of his voice. "You've got seconds, Monty! Or else he dies!"

Metres separated Remy and the agent providing the camera feed. His features became clearer as the distance narrowed with each step.

"Speak!"

Monty's countenance was unchanging. He bore no emotion, a fact that drew further rage from Maddox like nothing else could have done.

A single shot, the volume of which was tempered by the speakers around the oligarch's office, shattered the serenity of the park. Remy's dead body fell to the side, a fountain of blood spurting from the bullet hole in the back of his head and drenching the bench and the adjacent path. Maddox chuckled momentarily but he was quickly consumed again by voracious anger, fed by Monty's continued lack of reaction. The oligarch for Camden reached into a drawer on his desk and drew out a black Desert Eagle, pointing it shakily at Monty and striding to bring its barrel to his forehead.

"You want to die? Is that it? It wasn't enough, just watching your husband fucking perish, you want to go, too? I mean, that was going to happen anyways, but, well, hope is one hell of a drug, isn't it?"

"You're a madman," Monty seethed.

Maddox pressed the barrel further into Monty's forehead to the point where it began to hurt. "Maybe I am. But I'm a fucking powerful madman. I've got a vision and I've got the means to make it a reality, Monty. So really, it doesn't matter how sane you think I am. I can have whatever I want. I could kill you and throw your corpse from the window and there would be no consequences! Oh, here, watch this."

The gun fell from Monty's forehead as Maddox used it to gesture towards the screen, still streaming the body camera feed from the agent in the park. They strolled leisurely away from the chaos in a manner unbefitting of someone who had just committed murder in broad daylight. Police sirens sounded as vehicles arrived, blaring, to the boundaries of the park, officers streaming out of them and towards the agent with guns raised.

"This, now, watch this," Maddox emphasised gleefully.

The agent stopped walking as the officers barked orders for their surrender. They didn't surrender, a hand falling across the view of the camera as they presumably fished through their pocket for something. It wasn't immediately clear what that thing was as they found it and presented it to the police officers, but whatever it was, it prompted them to lower their weapons and allow passage.

"So you've paid off some police officers," Monty remarked. "Good for you. So have I. So has everyone else. Was this supposed to be special?"

"Have a closer look at the location for me," Maddox insisted. "Where is that?"

The agent turned around and provided a view of the path into the park from its gate. Monty's expression finally shifted as he registered recognition of the location.

"That's—"

"Victoria Park," Maddox finished. "In your very own Tower Hamlets. I'm not that dumb to think that paying off a couple police officers is unique, but they're not just any police officers, Monty. They're your police officers. Shall we have a look at Canary Wharf?"

The image on the screen shifted and the greenery was replaced by a panoramic view of the riverside and the reflective high-rise bearing the logo of the Sharpspace Corporation. There was no serene mundanity as had been the case in the park. Reams of mercenaries encircled crowds of executives and businesspeople huddled in small groups outside, SUVs with tinted windows and police cars parked at the possible exits from the walkway adjacent to the office block.

"I believe they're being apprehended. Your staff, that is," Maddox monologued. "I know they're being apprehended, actually, which will be because I ordered it."

"Nobody is going to stand for this," Monty choked. "You can't possibly believe you will survive this absurdity."

"I'll survive, don't you worry. Now, then, are you going to tell me about Vince Foster or will I have to scrape it off your chip?"

"You'll have to scrape me off the walls, too."

Maddox sighed sharply. "Fine."

The oligarch raised the gun and shot Monty in the head.

CHAPTER 32

When Noah had died, Vince knew immediately, owing to the fact that the pair had agreed to share a live feed of each other's vital monitors. That wasn't the case with Monty, and it was the news that first informed him of the oligarch's death. Or rather, disappearance.

The news notification that appeared on his HUD detailed an apparent corporate coup of the Sharpspace offices in Canary Wharf. Oliver Maddox was blamed as the initial suspect, and the oligarch soon personally claimed responsibility for the events as they unfolded. A call to Monty's chip went unanswered, and he didn't respond to any messages, either.

Vince found himself still in the PAL warehouse when the news broke, and he was quick to return to the meeting room where the leadership of the Camden Corps had broken into fervent discussion.

"You've seen what's happening?" Ava was the first to meet Vince at the door. "Maddox is going to start a bloody civil war. His forces are attacking Montgomery Sharp's offices right now. It doesn't look like there's any fighting, but there's no way that will be taken as anything other than a declaration of war."

"It's rather inconvenient," Vince mused. "Monty was my contact. And he's definitely dead."

"They haven't said that's the case yet."

"No, but I can't get a hold of him. We're going to have to rethink our plan."

"I've rethought it, and we're going right now," Ava declared. "We've been presented with a period of chaos and confusion. Oligarchs are going to be at each others' throats figuring out how to react to this. Maddox will be vulnerable in the fact that a significant portion of his security is busy deposing Montgomery Sharp. We go to the CSC headquarters now, guns blazing."

Commander Amini and the other leaders echoed words of assent and motioned towards the door, though Vince wasn't so eager. "We haven't had any time to prepare. Can you assemble a fighting force so rapidly?"

"Remember when I talked about decentralisation? Our fighting force is currently decentralised. It can very quickly become centralised. Maybe we haven't had a great deal of time to get ready, but we can't afford to waste this opportunity. It could be the best we ever get."

"Well, as long as you secure the roof and I can get inside first... it can work. But we have to work fast."

"We don't work any other way," Ava said confidently. "Are you coming with us?"

"No," Vince said. "I'll go there first myself and get into the building. I'll make my move after you arrive and the place gets put into lockdown."

The guerrilla leader nodded. "Good. Go now, then. We'll mobilise and meet at the building. You'll get a five-minute warning before we arrive."

Leaving the warehouse at pace, Vince put on his mask and sunglasses as well as purchasing a charcoal-grey flat cap from one of the many available stalls on his way out of the market.

The news only continued to break as he waited for a taxi to arrive at the street corner. A BBC livestream reported an outbreak of gunfire between what remained of Monty's security forces and the captors stationed outside the Sharpspace offices, a battle swiftly fought and won by Maddox's side.

Social media was set ablaze by the oligarchs' clashing responses to the events. Many of Maddox's inner-city allies rallied to his defence, in stark opposition to many of the oligarchs in control of the city's outer boroughs, who stood mostly united in their condemnation of the attack. Representatives of several world powers had also offered responses of their own by the time the taxi arrived, with condemnation coming in from the European, Japanese, Russian, and Australian presidents. The American president was oddly silent.

It was then that Vince realised he was in a race against the media to reach the headquarters of the Camden Space Corporation. He leaned forwards in the taxi and urged the driver to go faster, but it was a hopeless request in the face of the morning traffic. An unsettling anxiety washed over the hitman as he flicked his gaze between the unchanging surroundings and the map present on the car's dashboard screen. Despite its text being in a different language, it was easy to decipher the arrival time—several minutes later than Vince would have preferred.

The livestream continued to roll through his neural chip. Isobel Osborne issued a statement of her own offering veiled criticism of both sides while her mother came out in support of Montgomery Sharp. She promised to send what she described as a peacekeeping team into Canary Wharf, a provocation that Maddox himself spoke up to warn against. There was still no official news as to Monty's fate, though speculation had begun to circulate among those with connections to the oligarchy.

By the time Vince's taxi arrived at the offices of the CSC, he was one vehicle amongst a fleet. Vans from what must have been every news outlet in the city formed a blockade around the plaza while drones from beyond the reach of London swarmed like flies for a clear shot of the entrance. Some could be seen higher up in the air, tracing the building's perimeter in a sweeping search for what the hitman could only assume was Maddox.

Vince opened his phone and tapped a message to Ava with his exit onto the crowded pavement. *Abort the mission. Place is heaving with journalists.*

Her reply was immediate.

The mission is happening. This is your five minutes.

Vince clenched his fist and gritted his teeth, shoving his phone into his trouser pocket and gently fondling the handle of his pistol for reassurance.

There was a security presence outside the doors enough to handle the throng of voracious reporters, but the building didn't yet appear to be locked down. Employees filed neatly from the neighbouring block housing the building's private car park, flashing passes bearing the logo of the Camden Space Corporation. The guards forming a barricade between the entrance and the crowd filtered the workers between them, and that was all Vince needed to see to be able to formulate his next move.

A pathway from the centre of the plaza allowed access to the car park. The pedestrian entrance was locked, a keypad requiring one of the employee passes barring his way. The vehicle entrance, however, was not, and though barricades prevented access to unauthorised cars, there was nothing stopping Vince from walking out into the road and vaulting the barrier.

The hitman rushed through the reams of parked cars with long, hurried strides, scanning the area for a stairwell. He found one at the far end of the compound, employees making their ways routinely into and out of it, and headed towards it like a guided missile.

His victim was picked semi-randomly, though he wanted to be sure they wouldn't be able to fight back. That was the result he achieved. She didn't even have time to scream as he snatched her from the stairs and knocked her over the head with the butt of his pistol. Rendered immediately unconscious, Vince was able to rifle through her bag and steal the pass that he eventually found buried within it.

The guards didn't bat an eye at the distinctly different identities present on the pass and in the physical manifestation of the person bearing it, waving Vince quickly into the building where a furore had erupted over the uncertainty of the morning's developments. The hitman bypassed it entirely, making a beeline for the stairs despite the lifts continuing to function.

Seventy floors didn't sound insurmountable in his overconfident assumption of his own ability. That very quickly ceased to be his perception as he rose through the largely deserted and visually unremarkable stairwell at pace, opting to run in an attempt to make it as high as possible before the building went into lockdown. He found himself uncomfortably warm by the tenth floor, overheating by the fifteenth, and had left his coat behind by the twentieth, unholstering his pistol and clutching it in a sweaty hand as he continued his ascent.

Sirens blared as Vince sprinted, panting, past a sign bearing the number forty. It was at that point that the difficulty of his mission ratcheted up. A voice over a distant, echoing speaker announced the lockdown of the building and a repeating set of instructions for employees to make their way in an orderly manner towards the ground floor and subsequent basement.

What ensued was the very antithesis of an orderly manner as shaken employees streamed into the stairwell, proceeding to descend at a pace much quicker than that to which Vince had slowed in his fatigue. They mostly ignored the hitman, too caught up in their own panic to notice him. Those that did reflected confusion in their expressions, and when their eyes fell to the gun in his hand, they were quick to join the mob.

The crowd didn't stick to one side of the stairs. Vince was swamped from above as they fell upon him like a crashing wave, and he had to flatten himself to the railing to avoid being crushed.

His phone buzzed and he retrieved his phone with his free hand to read a barrage of messages from Ava.

We have people on the roof.

They're fighting his security forces.

They won't last forever.

But they should be able to disable his escape helicopter.

The mass of people began to thin and Vince pushed his way through them to continue up the stairs.

Commander Amini is with the forces we landed on the roof.

He'll message you if they have an update on Maddox.

The hitman reached the fiftieth floor and there was no sign of security personnel or otherwise.

Vince.

This is Amini.

Maddox has gone into the building.

His security has mostly stayed back to fight.

The last few stragglers were making their way down as Vince began to hear gunshots from the firefight taking place on the roof. He brushed past a sign labelled 55. The building vibrated softly with an explosion from above and screams from below.

Maddox's voice bellowed down the stairwell with complete absence of restraint. "Could someone please explain to me why there are communists fucking everywhere?"

The hitman exchanged his pistol into his left hand to wipe his sweaty palm dry before returning it to his right and aiming it at the now empty stairs above him. Though the firefight continued in the background, it was the thunderous footsteps of the approaching security force that produced the greatest volume.

A click to Vince's right signalled what appeared to be the death of both him and his chance to eliminate Maddox. "Drop your weapon," the guard spoke, materialising from the doorway to the offices adjacent and training their gun to meet Vince's exposed side. The hitman gingerly lowered himself to the floor, raising his hands above his head as the stampeding footsteps grew continuously louder.

The group of security forces with Maddox at their centre arrived, providing the perfect cover for Vince to pivot and face the only guard paying him any heed. They passed between the two in their distracted hurry and Vince fired once in the moment that appeared. He took a bullet himself, but that was in his shoulder. His opponent fell backwards with a messy wound adorning their forehead.

Maddox's security may have been noisy, but the exchange of gunfire in the enclosed space was ear-splitting. There was a terse set of comments from the guards as some of them turned around and one that wasn't so terse from Maddox, who carried on down with the rest. Vince took shelter in the indent housing the door to the offices, aiming at the space where the guards would arrive. When they did, he took one free shot and then turned tail, opening the door behind him and sprinting madly for further cover.

The series of desks and dividers that ensued couldn't have been more perfect. He ducked behind one and waited for the guards to burst into the room, and when they did, he took another free shot. Those who didn't fall returned fire, but the hitman had already moved on.

Wood splintered and glass shattered, fabric ripped and electronics fizzed. Bullets flew everywhere, unleashed without discrimination. Vince wove through the maze of screens and took down another guard firing blindly in the wrong direction. He heard the shouts of two or three more, converging from all around upon the site of their fallen companion.

"Come out!" one of them shouted, their collective gunfire momentarily ceasing.

The hitman intended to do no such thing and took shelter behind a section of divider that hadn't been obliterated in the bodyguards' rampage. He heard their measured steps towards the body and tempered his own breathing, keen to maintain his absolute composure. Searing pain burned in the wound in his shoulder, hot blood acting as glue against his sodden shirt.

He reached into his pocket for his phone, wincing, and tapped a message to Commander Amini with one hand. *I need help on floor 55.* And then with a suppressed grunt he returned the device to his pocket and clutched his pistol to his face with both hands as the footsteps drew closer.

Patience played to Vince's advantage once more as another guard moved into his view and subsequently fell dead with the ringing out of his gun. He didn't waste a moment in bolting as the tenuous truce fell apart in an instant.

Bullets whizzed past the hitman's head as they continued to pepper every stray surface in the office. He clambered over a series of desks and chairs, leaving them spinning in his wake, and manoeuvred back towards the exit to the stairwell. An exposed stretch of ground separated him from it and the torn fabric of the surrounding dividers revealed guards closing in from both sides. They caught sight of Vince in the same moment that he did them, but it also happened to be the same moment that a bright stream of red flowed through the doorway and opened fire in turn with the guards.

The PAL fighters provided the barrier needed to pass safely into the stairwell, their weapons erupting upon the outnumbered security guards. Commander Amini was quick to notice Vince's crippled shoulder, laying a hand gently upon it but being batted away by the irascible hitman as he forged onwards, eyes unabatedly set upon the stairs down.

"Vince!" Amini grabbed him more firmly on the shoulder not decorated by a bullet wound. "You can't go on with a hit like that."

"Maddox is on these stairs right now," Vince seethed, attempting to twist away and struggling against both Amini's powerful grip and the cutting pain from his shoulder. "These bodyguards we've put down are nothing compared to what he has coming. If I don't get down there right now, he will escape and we will be slaughtered. All of us."

The guerrilla drew and cocked his pistol. "Then I'll go get him."

"No." Vince reached up with his free hand and nauseating effort. "He's mine."

"Don't be selfish," Amini growled. "What matters is that he dies. For the collective good. I know you might not care about that, but unfortunately for you, it's one of our main beliefs. So get yourself onto the roof, where one of our helicopters is waiting, and go back to base to get treatment."

"Look, these grunts might listen to your every word, but you don't control me. I'm going to go kill Maddox. You can come with me if you want, but the final bullet better come from my gun."

"You'll be lucky if you make it down the stairs. We're coming in from the ground floor, too, you know? Chances are Ava's troops will find him before either of us do. And they aren't going to wait to let you have the glory. Have some fucking sense."

"I'm going to kill Maddox," Vince spat once more before escaping Amini's grasp and ploughing towards the stairs.

Each step came with a crippling jolt of pain but the hitman was undeterred, powered by pride and lust for revenge in equal measure. Amini followed behind him, a motion Vince both appreciated and resented. His progress down was no faster than it had been going up, hampered by a necessitated clinging to the railing. A thin trail of blood trickled down from his shoulder and onto the floor and he felt dizzy, uncertain. He stepped forwards, too far. The pain that had become rhythmic in its pattern exploded as he fell and tumbled almost to the floor, caught at the last moment by a keen-eyed Commander Amini who gently lowered him into a sitting position.

"You can't go on like this."

Vince groaned in a strained effort to lean forward. "I've had it worse. I will keep going."

"If it means that much to you then I will make sure nobody kills him. Then you can have all the glory you want." Amini pulled a walkie-talkie from his belt. "Ava. Are you inside the building?"

"We've captured a load of hostages on the ground floor but we've taken losses," the guerrilla leader's voice crackled back.

"Vince has taken a hit. He wants to go after Maddox but frankly, he's not in a state to do that. I've told him I won't let any of us kill him."

"So what are you saying? Vince wants us to—on the rare chance that we might come face to face with our biggest

261

enemy—let him live so that he can carry out his personal vendetta? Is he there with you now?"

Amini held the walkie-talkie down to Vince's head and pressed the button for him.

"Yes," Vince said wincingly. "I'm here."

"I've got some tough news for you, Vince. We don't do heroes in PAL. You wanted to kill him yourself? Shouldn't have got yourself shot. If we see Maddox, every single person is on shoot-to-kill orders. You understand?"

Vince shot a glance at Amini, refraining from pressing the button to talk to Ava. "I'm getting up and carrying on if you can't stop her."

"Nobody can stop her, Vince," Amini sighed, sliding his hands into his pockets and looking up towards the ceiling. "I've never met anyone more stubborn in my life. But she's the boss, so we do what she says."

"Help me up." The hitman grimaced as he pressed himself from the floor with one arm.

"You carry on like this and you'll end up with permanent damage to that shoulder. If you haven't got it already."

Vince offered a wry smile and laughed, anticipating entirely the look of disapproval he knew would follow. "I don't think so. I've got real good insurance."

CHAPTER 33

"Maria, my building has been flooded with fucking communists and my army is all busy taking over Sharpspace. What little is left of my personal security is either with me or on their way, but it's not going to be enough. I'm out-numbered—I need more. Whatever American troops you've got lying around, I need you to send them to the CSC offices. Heavily armed, preferably."

Maddox thundered down the stairs amidst the protective cocoon of bodyguards shielding every facet of him. Despite it, he didn't feel very safe, and he found himself consistently annoyed at the slow speed at which they had to descend so as not to trip over one another. His holstered Desert Eagle thumped routinely against his hip with each step.

"What the fuck are we even doing?" the oligarch then exclaimed more generally, lowering the phone from his ear but remaining on the call. "We've got drones, where are they?"

He turned and shoved the bodyguard behind him to the side without any care to maintain formation.

"Sir, I really wouldn't go back up there," the guard protested. "They're on the fiftieth floor and we're a couple guards down."

"Where are my fucking drones?" Maddox persisted, not paying the bodyguard much attention as he drew his pistol from its holster and gesticulated to emphasise his fervour.

"What drones, sir?" a different guard questioned impatiently.

"My new drones. My fucking killer death machine drones. I paid through the fucking nose for them so where the fuck were they when I needed them?"

The guards exchanged glances reflecting equal parts uncertainty and bewilderment while the oligarch returned his attention back to the phone.

"Maria, my drones. I ordered them from a company you recommended. Where are they?"

"I don't know, Oliver. But I've been trying to tell you, they won't do what you're asking. They need a human pilot. Get yourself to safety."

"Are you sending troops?"

"I have no troops to send. The President is in charge of the army and I have no remit to ask him to send in what we do have in London to reinforce your coup."

"They're not reinforcing my coup, they're fighting off a fucking communist uprising! Pull some strings, for God's sake!"

Distant shouts and indiscernible crashes and bangs echoed up the airy stairwell.

"There's not enough time," Maria reiterated, maintaining utterly calm.

"Definitely not when you keep yammering on! I need assistance, Maria, or you will lose your one connection to a city I know you've got a great deal invested in. If they've come after me, they will find out about you and come after everything you own. Not to mention that your career will be done for when the press finds out that you've been going behind your own president's back to forge alliances. Is that enough motivation, Maria?"

The ground shook with the force of a distant explosion, dust falling gently from the ceiling.

Maddox turned his attention back to his bodyguards. "There is no point going down there. There will be more of them down there than there were upstairs."

"If we go upstairs we'll be massacred," one guard protested. "Just like everybody else already has been."

"We go downstairs and we're the subject of a blind, angry mob," the oligarch argued. "There are less upstairs. Upstairs, I have a chance at negotiating. All I need is time."

The guards' crumbling professionalism exhibited itself in their hesitation to follow any particular course of action. They wavered as Maddox took heavy, predetermined steps back in the direction from which they had come, prompting a look so fiery it felt as if lasers might beam from the oligarch's eyes.

Maddox stormed further ahead, followed by the guards as they reluctantly decided it to be their only viable option. Though voices echoed all around as the forces of the PAL converged, it was the oligarch's that rang out the loudest. He called out all manner of instructions, questions, and plain obscenities as it became clearer and clearer that he wasn't going to find the time he so desperately coveted.

"Just hide, Oliver." Maria had long grown accustomed to Maddox's angry outbursts, though never had they taken place in a situation so dire as that which had taken hold. "It's a huge building. You can hide and they won't find you before your forces get there."

"Hide like a rat?" Maddox spat. "I've just incited a coup. I'm not about to run and hide! What kind of leader would do that?"

The politician's patience finally faltered. "One that wants to survive, for God's sake! Don't try to be a hero, because you're far from that. You're a drugged-up psycho with a lot of money and with it, a lot of power and a lot of enemies."

Maddox carried on.

"You've been in power long enough to know that you can spin the story however you like as long as you're still alive to tell it," Maria continued, though Maddox had stopped listening. He turned the corner onto the fortieth floor and found himself face-to-face with two individuals, their guns bearing down upon the group as it ascended.

Vince was a mess, a stark deterioration from the neatly groomed man that had come to meet him in his office not that long ago. His hair was matted with a mixture of sweat and blood, a trail of the latter streaming from his shoulder and leaving a sticky streak down his shirt. His chest expanded and contracted with exhausted breaths, and yet plastered across his face was a grimace that managed to somehow reflect smug victory.

It was impossible to perceive what followed. Maddox's ears rang with the eruption of gunfire and he was able to discharge a single bullet before falling amidst the volley of projectiles flying in both directions.

Maria shrieked shrilly over the phone that had fallen to the ground and shattered. Maddox thrust away the body of one of his guards as it fell atop him and elicited the discharge of blood from the back of his throat. He looked to the hand that held his gun and tried to raise it but was met with the boot of a man who he vainly hoped was one of his guards tripping over him. When he looked up, he found the man's jacket to be a desaturated cherry-red.

The man leaned down to pick up the shattered phone, grunting subtly in the process. He said nothing as Maria continued to babble. Maddox couldn't make out a word of it, his ears still ringing as another globule of blood pooled in the back of his throat and forced him to cough.

He couldn't see Vince. It became apparent that he wouldn't be able to sit up with whatever damage had been done in the seconds that had passed. And then he could see Vince. The hitman came to stand over him, torso and leg adorned with a pair of new bullet wounds but his gun ever present in his hand. He had to be supported by the other man to avoid falling over.

The oligarch smirked and tried to speak but first had to cough up another round of blood. "I—"

Vince didn't allow him any more than that.

CHAPTER 34

Amini handed the phone to Vince silently, but Vince didn't even need to look at it to know who was on the other end. Her raspy voice was recognisable despite the distortion by the phone's damaged speakers.

The button to hang up was inaccessible through the cracked screen, so Vince tossed the phone to rest atop Maddox's eviscerated body. Then he collapsed himself.

He hadn't expected to see Ava's face when he later awoke and yet that was exactly who stood at the end of the bed. It was quiet—there was nothing in the way of the constant ruckus that had existed before he fell unconscious, only the dull humming and intermittent beeping of hospital machines.

A cannula fed blood into his right arm and his eyes swept alarmedly over the rest of the room. It was only him and the guerrilla leader present and the sole window to the outside was glazed over and tinted.

"Where are we?" the hitman asked.

Ava turned to look at him. "Not London, obviously. You'd have been dead a good while ago. Amini was kind enough to take you across the border himself, and then some. You're not special, though. We won't be going back to London for a while."

"What's happened?"

"What hasn't happened?" Ava rolled her eyes and gazed off towards the other side of the room, a slight, amused smile creasing her face. "After you had your moment of glory, of course. Well, where to begin? Maddox is dead and his little insurrection is suddenly without a ringleader. There's nobody obvious familywise for his empire to pass to and he didn't leave a will. Even if he had done, his allies aren't about to wait for the legal wrangling. They're already squabbling over who gets what and you would have thought that that'd mean they're too busy to worry about us, but oh, no. They declared open war on us the moment it was discovered Maddox had been killed. Bad news for you, I'm afraid. They caught you on camera fighting alongside us. In their eyes, you are a communist. You are an enemy of the people, and you will not hide in London for as long as the oligarchy lives."

Vince sighed. "What are you going to do, then?"

"Lay low for a while. That's what we do best. And then fight back. We're at war now, so that's expected, right?

The fish rots from the head and we've already cut off one. What's another thirty?"

She turned back around to look at Vince with an expectant gleam in her eyes. "But what about you? Now that you're publicly associated with the People's Army, you surely can't expect to go back to hitman work? Every other client will be a sting."

"I know some good face surgeons. And I have plenty of identities I'm yet to go through."

Ava's tone was laced with insistence as she continued. "That can't be a life worth living. You've got money. More than you'll ever need. What are you even working for at that point? Don't you want to build something? A legacy? Something to leave behind when you're gone? Change the world in some way? Or are you really satisfied just going on and making more money? Because I'm sorry, but I don't see how that can be fulfilling in any way."

"It's a good thing we're different people, then," Vince quipped.

"Fight with us, Vince." This time, the insistence wasn't suggestive as the guerrilla impressed the hitman's chest with her hands. "Even if it's for yourself. Even if I can't convince you to do it for the cause. You will look over your shoulder for the rest of your days if the oligarchy isn't destroyed. And don't give me some bullshit 'I already look over my shoulder'—this is not the same. If you have the might of an entire world power hunting you down, they will find you, wherever you hide. And they will exterminate you without mercy. Your death would be celebrated. Is that really the future you want for yourself? Or do you want to do something about it? And maybe, just maybe, you could think about the people you'd be helping?"

A nurse entered the room and there was a period of silence underscored by tensions so taut that Vince felt physically restrained. Ava held his gaze for the lengthy disposal of the empty blood bag and dismantling of the cannula. She held it still as they were returned to privacy.

"Well?" she seethed.

Vince stood up and uncomfortably flexed his arm, wincing but feeling generally free of pain. "It's not the right thing for me. Sorry. How long have I been here?"

"They put you into a coma to stop sepsis setting in. That was a month ago. Where are you going? You can't leave yet."

"I'll come back." Vince searched through a bag next to the door containing all his possessions, including his loaded pistol, but only took his phone. "But there's something I have to do first."

CHAPTER 35

The digital bell chimed as Vince crossed into the gun shop, having travelled back into London under the name Linus Aberg. He had also cut his hair and kept the scraggly beard that had emerged during his coma.

"Good evening." He had somewhat expected the shopkeeper to recognise him, but that wasn't immediately the case. "I need something subtle."

The shopkeeper glanced around the shop as if surveying the rest of the customers, of which there were none. "How subtle?"

"Pass-through-airport-security subtle."

It was at that point that the shopkeeper met Vince's eyes and a spark of recognition flashed across his countenance. Not just from his earlier business, but from his outdated face plastered across every news outlet in the city-state. "I know you."

"And I'm hoping we can keep that between ourselves."

The shopkeeper looked down at a tablet built into the counter and tapped a series of buttons resulting in an audible click as the front door locked.

"I may have something," he proceeded to say coyly. "But it's going to be expensive. Real expensive."

"Show me."

With a swift gesture Vince was ushered through a door behind the counter into a dingy back room, walls lined with racks and racks of weapons, ammunition, and other varyingly lethal paraphernalia. The light strips along the ceiling beamed out in differing shades of white and yellow with inconsistent intensities. It was bone-chillingly cold.

"I take it the last one I sold you met its intended application," the shopkeeper exclaimed, leading Vince past tables littered with stray bullets, rifle attachments, and their accompanying frames.

"It did, but I didn't buy it for what you've seen on the news," Vince mused, surprised at his own nonchalance. "This, though, whatever you're about to show me—this is for something specific."

"Okay, well, hear me out before you bin it off."

The shopkeeper pulled a dusty plastic bin out from beneath a cluttered worktop. Whatever he was looking for wasn't the only thing in it as he spent a good while rustling through its myriad contents with a series of inquisitive exclamations and frustrated grumblings.

"Here's one part." An object resembling the barrel of a pistol was placed onto the worktop, though it had a texture resembling carbon fibre. It was soon joined by a frame, a trigger, and eventually the rest of the parts that would have been necessary to construct the entire weapon, all in the same black colour and sleek texture. "And that's all of them."

"3D-printed," Vince remarked, recognising the technique used to build the weapons of choice of the gangs of London prior to its declaration of independence and subsequent liberalisation of firearm laws. "I know for a fact that these are cheap as chips to produce. What makes it expensive?"

"You know what makes it expensive," the shopkeeper quipped. "I've been holding onto this for a while. It's carbon fibre composite. No metal parts, not even the pin. It'll still fire, but only once. Get it through the metal detector in pieces, go to the loo, whatever, and then make it count. I wouldn't just sell this to anyone—it's for a very specific subset of customers."

"You don't know me at all."

"I know enough."

Vince picked up a few of the pieces and ran his finger over them with a curious look. "What's the charge?"

"Fifty grand," the shopkeeper said without missing a beat.

The hitman paid and left the shop before the transaction had cleared.

CHAPTER 36

"Miss Sanchez! Miss Sanchez! How does the U.S. plan to respond to the void of leadership in London?"

"Miss Sanchez! What does the U.S. know about the assassination of the London oligarchs?"

"Miss Sanchez! Does the U.S. government intend to intervene to defeat the communist uprising in London?"

Flashing lights. Dimmed by neural chip plugins the Secretary of State had installed long ago, but nonetheless constant. And though they might have been hidden from her perception, they still existed in the way they drenched her in white for the rest of the world to see.

It was nothing new. Maria lived for it.

"Good evening," she began, the rowdy crowd of journalists wrangled into relative silence by the security presence. "I want to begin by saying that the position of the government of the United States remains firm. We condemn entirely the assassination of members of the London leadership and any acts of violence by communist terrorists. Our hearts go out to those affected and we would like to reassure them once again that the United States is utilising all diplomatic channels available to bring about peace to the City of London."

She paused for a moment to breathe and that was enough for the expected clamouring to erupt. She waited patiently for quiet before resuming.

"The United States is working directly with the United Republic and the Federated States to draft a resolution to the ongoing crisis. It is not our intention to intervene militarily but if citizens or assets of the United States are threatened, we will consider any means to protect them.

"As we have already published, the individual behind the assassination of Oliver Maddox has been identified as Vince Foster, a hitman working in the ranks of the London communists. Our intelligence services are working together with those of our international partners day and night to track him down and bring him to justice, as well as searching to secure the identity of the individual behind the assassination of Montgomery Sharp. They, too, will then face justice.

"These events are tragic and stark reminder of the fact that the world we now live in remains ever unstable. There are a great many people and factions who wish to exploit this instability to achieve their goals, political or otherwise. We cannot afford to be weak in the face of this threat. So this is the message of the United States to all those who would threaten the fragile peace we achieved in the face of catastrophic adversity—we will not bow. We will not be deterred and we will defeat every enemy to democracy that chooses to stand in our way.

"But the situation in London is not all I am here to talk about today. It's also of the utmost importance that I address—"

The running of the tap in the toilets was a serene white noise occupying the drowning silence to which Maria escaped after the conference. It was in front of the mirror that she stood for some time, allowing the swirling thoughts that so permanently raged through her head to dissipate and settle. She closed her eyes and focused on her breathing. They couldn't be silenced, but they could be sidelined, at least for a little while.

She eventually rejoined the corridor still host to journalists from every outlet in the country. They had a look to them, the same eyes and smiles and neat, corporate haircuts. One didn't, and he caught her eye. It seemed to her that he was trying to. She looked down at his hands and saw the gun he brandished and by that point it was too late.

CHAPTER 37

"Who the hell is knocking at this hour? Why didn't they just buzz us?"

"I have no idea. I'll go get it."

Ruth groaned and stepped out of bed, pulling on her underwear from the floor, wrapping herself in a dressing gown, and resignedly rubbing her forehead. Her hair was a mess and there were bags under her eyes and she was really very disappointed to have been torn from her bed.

Noah hadn't messaged in a while. She could almost bear it when he was away for months at a time but still maintained digital contact, but recent times had been the last straw. She had tried to call him after weeks of silence and eventually had to resort to an angry text which, if read receipts were to be believed, hadn't even been viewed.

"I'm coming!" she snapped as the knocking from the front door reverberated through the flat once more. She was about to unleash an angry tirade upon her midnight visitor but held her tongue as the door slid open and she laid her eyes upon a man that bore a remarkable resemblance to that which had occupied every news station earlier that day.

"Hello, Ruth," he said mutedly. "I apologise for intruding at this time. My flight got in an hour ago and I can't stay."

"Vince." Ruth felt herself immediately racked by the urge to sob but restrained herself for the sake of staying quiet. "I...I don't—"

And then she was angry. The internalised fury she had for so long directed at her absent boyfriend boiled over in a sudden surge of rage that she unleashed without restraint upon this man she had only ever known in passing. "Tell me the truth, Vince! Where is he? What is he? What are you? I have had it up to here with being forced to live like this. It's not living. I don't get to experience things in the way that everyone else does. I don't get to have my happy ending. I just have to go on pretending that I'm content with devoting myself to someone who's never even here and I'm not even sure I know who they are. I don't doubt that Noah loves me but there needs to be more than that. I can't... I can't..."

The sobs that had fought to escape won their battle and she fell into Vince's shoulder. The hitman wrapped an arm around her and stifled a grunt as a sharp pain shot through his still-healing wound. A man dressed less modestly than Ruth emerged from the living room with a gaze that Vince would at first have described as curiosity, before progressing into perplexity and then alarm. He held eye contact and could almost read the man's thoughts as he ran through his options in his head before eventually deciding, smartly, to return to bed.

"Why are you here, Vince?" Ruth finally withdrew her head. The bags under her eyes were soaked.

"I'm very sorry." Vince joined Ruth in crying as tears formed in his own eyes. "Noah won't be coming back."

It was as if he'd struck her in the gut. Her countenance was deprived of any angry resolve as she collapsed, crestfallen, back into the hitman's arms. She didn't know what to think. When she did try to think, nothing compiled itself in any sort of logical order. Only a jumbled mess of emotions over which she had very little in the way of control.

They both cried—Ruth perhaps more vigorously, but Vince harder than he had ever done in his life.

He was the first to regain his composure. "It's likely that the police will question you because of your association with Noah and therefore me. You will tell them everything you know. Do not feel the need to protect me."

He felt her nod into the nook of his arm.

"And I'm sorry, but I need to go now."

"Why? Can you at least tell me that?"

"Because I'm wanted in the entirety of the civilised world. I'm especially wanted in the City of London. I'm jeopardising my safety with every extra minute I spend within these borders. And I need to get back to the hospital. I was shot in the shoulder and left before I could heal properly."

Ruth took a weary step backwards. "Thank you. Thank you for coming and telling me."

"It's what he wanted. Goodbye, Ruth."

The hitman stepped out and watched the door slide closed. Through its opaque surface he could still make out Ruth's shadowy figure, joined shortly thereafter by that of the man he had seen earlier. They exchanged a few words and Vince took that as his cue to leave.

He took his phone out of his pocket and called a specific contact. It was far too late to expect her to pick up, but she did anyways.

"What do you want, Vince? What fucking time do you call this?"

"I've changed my mind," the hitman declared. "I'll fight with you."

END OF BOOK ONE